Mountain Man Daddy Series

Mountain Man Doctor (Book 3)

S.E. Riley

The Redherring Publishing House

Mountain Man Doctor (Book 3)

TRIGGER WARNING

This book contains mentions of alcohol addiction, relapse, and recovery.

Table of Contents

Prologue

Naomi

Ten years away from home had never felt so awful.

When I was seventeen, I moved away from Blopton Town and never looked back. Back then, life in a small town had seemed overrated. I was young and wanted to live in a city where nobody knew my name or my parents. I wanted to build a life far away from the sleepy little mountain town.

Now that I was back, I have no clue why I had left.

As I ran, I inhaled the scent of the forest and felt the tension leave my body. The carnage that had become my life started to fade away with each new twist in the trail I took.

My footsteps were steady, and my heart was racing as I came to a stop in front of one of the giant redwoods. The trees towered over me, their leaves littering the ground as fall ravaged the forest.

The trail split into two just ahead of me. To the right was a path I had run a thousand times as a teenager. To the left was a newer path that hadn't been filled with woodchips yet.

I stretched out my legs for a second before I took off towards the new path, eager to explore the new section of the forest. More leaves coated the ground, hiding the path from sight. I kept running in a relatively straight line, dodging rocks and jumping over roots.

Lately, running was the only thing that cleared my mind.

Suddenly, the ground was falling out beneath my feet. I screamed as I fell. A root caught my crop top, ripping it as I plummeted to the bottom of the hole. My ankle twisted as I landed, jerking hard and sending me to my knees.

Tears blurred my vision as I looked around.

Why the hell is there a trap in the middle of a fucking running path? I thought as I tried to stand.

The pain that shot through my ankle was unbearable. I screamed and fell back down, clutching my ankle. Even in the relative darkness of the hole, I could see that my ankle was swollen.

"Help!" I shouted, wishing that I had brought my phone.

The phone was sitting on the dining table in my parents' house, waiting for me to come back. I hadn't wanted anything in the tiny pocket of my shorts while I ran, but apparently, that had been a mistake.

"Help!"

Without being able to put any weight on my ankle, I couldn't climb out of the hole. I scowled and glared up at the leaves falling on me. There was nothing I could do now but shout and hope that somebody would run through this trail like I did.

I shouted until my voice was hoarse before I heard the crunching of leaves near the hole. When I shouted again, the crunching grew louder until it stopped, and a man was looking down at me.

"Please help," I said. "My ankle's hurt, and I can't get out of here."

His lips twitched slightly at my predicament. "Can you move to one side? I'm going to jump down and lift you out."

I scrambled to press myself as close to one side of the hole as possible. The man landed beside me and grinned. That smile knocked the air from my lungs as I stared at him, his eyes the color of sea glass regarding me warmly.

"Hey," he said, crouching down to scoop me up.

He was careful not to hit my ankle as he lifted me higher, placing me on the edge of the hole. I scrambled backward using my hands and good ankle while he lifted himself out of the hole.

"Thank you," I said, staring up at him and trying to ignore how his hands on my body filled my stomach with butterflies.

"I can take you down to the clinic and fix up your ankle," he said. He crouched down and held out his hand. "Dr. Zane Morrin."

"Addie Manning."

"You're okay with me carrying you, right? It's going to be the fastest way to get you to my truck."

"If it means I can have pain meds sooner, go for it."

He laughed and picked me up again, avoiding my ankle. I didn't know what to do with my arms while he carried me, so I settled for looping one around his shoulders and trying to keep myself upright as he walked over the bumpy trail.

The drive from the trailhead to the clinic was short and slightly awkward. Zane made small talk about nothing in particular while I gritted my teeth against the pain. He had given me some pain medication when he got to his truck and wrapped my ankle, but it still wasn't enough to kill the dull ache.

When he carried me into the clinic, I could feel the eyes on us. The man sitting behind the desk smirked as he answered a phone call. My cheeks were burning as he carried me into one of the exam rooms and shut the door behind us.

"Do you have anyone who can come and get you?" he asked.

"Yeah. I can call my mom if you have a phone I can borrow."

"We'll get you one," he said as he took off the wrapping. "Now, let's take a look at that ankle."

He made quick work of the exam, his fingers skating over my skin and sending shivers down my spine. I kept ignoring the butterflies in my stomach as he worked, trying to remind myself that he was just doing his job.

Once my ankle was wrapped, and I was given a pair of crutches, he escorted me out of the office with strict instructions to stay off my ankle. When my mom's car came speeding around the corner, I grinned.

"That's her. Thank you for all your help."

"Addie, what happened?" my mom asked as soon as she put the car in park and walked around to the passenger side. "Is it anything serious, Zane?"

Zane? Did they know each other?

"Nothing lots of rest won't fix…" he said as he helped me into the car.

"Zane, you're needed…" the man who had been behind the desk called out from the door before disappearing back inside.

"Oh, thank God," Mom said as she buckled my seat.

"Gosh, Mom, it's just a sprain…I'll be fine." Mom kissed my forehead before closing the door and rounding the car to the driver's side.

"Keep off the ankle, Addie," he said as he opened the door to the clinic, ready to head back inside. "And call the office later to make a follow-up appointment. I need to make sure that you're taking care of yourself and not doing any more damage."

When the door closed behind him, I finally let out the breath I had been holding. Trying to forget the feeling of his hands on my body would be impossible.

Chapter 1

Zane

I ran a hand through my hair as I finished filling out the notes on my patient's chart. There was no shortage of elderly people coming in, searching for some sort of new medication they could try for a problem they had made up. Though the visits were always long, they kept my day moving. I couldn't fault any of them for looking for something to do.

Hell, I was lonely too. I wanted someone to talk to, and the never-ending line of the elderly provided me with the companionship of some form, even if it was in a completely professional capacity.

There was a knock at the door before my office administrator, Van, stuck his head in the door with a grin. I waved him in and set my notes to the side.

"What's going on?" I asked as his grin grew wider.

"So," Van said, dropping into one of the leather chairs on the other side of my desk. "I noticed that you haven't made a follow-up appointment with Addie Manning yet. Aren't you worried about how her ankle is healing?"

I rolled my eyes and leaned back in the chair. Van was young, and hiring him had been more because of his mother's begging than his actual qualifications—though he had gone to school to be a medical office administrator. However, he kept me on my toes and kept me entertained. He was one of the few people in town who treated me like a normal person instead of someone to talk about.

Still, I didn't like that he was asking about Addie. It meant that he had seen the way I stared at her for a few seconds too long as she left the clinic after every visit.

"And since when do you keep tabs on who's been in the office recently and who hasn't?" I asked. "I've seen her a few times in the last three weeks to check on her ankle, but they've been brief appointments. You would know that if you kept on top of the filing."

Van waved a hand and smirked. "That's a job for another day. Why don't we talk about how irritated you are that she rushes in here and rushes out without giving you the time of day? I've heard it's hard on an aging man's ego."

"I'm only thirty-seven," I said, gritting my teeth as I sat up and started working on my notes again. Thirty-seven wasn't old, but it wasn't young anymore, either. He didn't need to remind me about my age.

With everything that I had been through in my life, thirty-seven felt ancient some days.

"You ignored what I said about Addie, though. That's interesting. If you want, I can go find her file and get her address so you can make a house call."

"That's a massive violation of patient privacy," I said, looking up from my paperwork and fixing him with a stern look. "Please tell me that you aren't doing that."

"Are you kidding me? Mom would have my head." Van shuddered. "She's making you all kinds of fruit preserves for Christmas."

"She really doesn't have to do that," I said, wondering what I would do with fruit preserves. I lived alone, and there was no need to have multiple jars.

"You don't understand. She really does have to. You splinted the cat's leg and gave her baby boy a job. She talks about you all the time."

I groaned and ran a hand down my face. I knew that even after five years in Blopton, I was still a gossip topic among the townspeople. Lately, it had more to do with my relationship status than anything else. It seemed like most of the mothers thought that the only doctor in a small town would be the perfect husband for their daughter.

They didn't know the skeletons that liked to live in my closet. Otherwise, they might have thought differently.

Not a week went by where there wasn't a well-meaning woman who offered me her daughter's number or who gave me their own. All those numbers ended up in the garbage as soon as I got home. I wasn't interested in settling down with anybody.

They wouldn't understand me.

I was uninterested in finding a relationship, at least until I saw Addie. There was something about her that drew me in and held me captive. I wanted to know more about her. I wanted her to be the first person I let into my life in a long time.

It scared the hell out of me.

"Honestly," Van said, shaking his head. "If I have to hear one more story about you, I'm going to go insane."

The phone started ringing before Van could tell me exactly what his mother had been saying about me lately. I glanced at him, but he made no move to go answer the phone.

With a sigh, I picked up the receiver. "Hello, Morrin Medical. Dr. Morrin speaking."

"Hi, Zane," Fleur Manning said, her soft French accent lilting. "Would you mind going to Addie's apartment? She just called me and said that she fell in the shower and her ankle hurts too much to get up. I've tried to lift her, but with the way my back's been hurting lately, I can't."

As much as I wanted to say no, Fleur was my neighbor. She and her husband, Alex, had welcomed me with open arms when I moved to town and caught me up on everything I might need to know while living in Blopton. They invited me over for weekly dinners, and it wasn't uncommon for Fleur to show up on my doorstep with leftovers from their dinner.

"I'll be over as soon as I can, Fleur. Where does Addie live?"

"Those apartments on Main Street. Number five. I'll meet you at the door and let you in."

In the background, I could hear Addie ask her mother who she was talking to. Fleur said something in French before ending the call. I sighed and got up, grabbing a bag filled with supplies.

"And where might you be going in such a hurry?" Van asked, a smirk already forming. "You look like you're off on an important mission. A house call, maybe?"

"Get back to work, and don't worry about what I'm doing," I said before leaving the office.

As much as Van liked to tease me, I knew he wouldn't say anything to anyone about where I was going or what I was doing. He might have only been twenty-six, but he had enough sense to know that some things in this town didn't need repeating.

I loaded my bag into the backseat of the truck and got in. My clinic sat just outside of town by the forest. It was the perfect location for someone who loved the woods but didn't want the townspeople dropping in to chat on their way by. I had work to get down on and couldn't spend much time chatting.

Packing my bags and moving to Blopton five years ago had been an impulsive decision at best. It was exactly the kind of decision that I had been told to avoid making. But I didn't regret making that move, especially when I didn't have that many options to begin with. Getting this clinic had been a welcome surprise. The location was the main reason why I purchased it. I didn't think I would get back into practicing medicine after taking an extended break. I thought I was done with that, but then I saw the little clinic for sale nearly three years ago, and everything fell into place.

Heading into town always left an uneasy feeling. It felt like people were watching me and waiting for me to make a mistake. Living on the outskirts of town and avoiding the drama was easier.

As I drove, I drummed my fingers on the wheel and tried not to think about what I was headed to do. There was a good chance that Addie was still going to be naked when I was there. I had seen plenty of naked patients in my career but being attracted to the patient was entirely new for me.

I won't be acting like a horny teenage boy, no matter how long it's been since I've been with someone, I thought as I turned off the dirt road that led to the clinic and onto the only paved road that led to town from the clinic.

I was going to get to Addie's, and I was going to be professional. I would pretend that I wasn't attracted to her, and everything would be alright. It would only take a few minutes to get her out of the tub, check her ankle, and leave again.

Neither of us would be more uncomfortable than we had to be.

At least, I hoped that we wouldn't be.

Chapter 2

Addie

"I can't believe you called the doctor," I said as I glared at my mom from where I was sitting in the tub. "That isn't necessary. I would have been able to get myself out of here eventually."

"Well, it was either the doctor or your father since you don't have any male friends in town, and I couldn't lift you. I thought that I picked the best option given the situation," Mom said with a slight shrug and a sly smile before murmuring something in French and walking away.

It was then that I wished I had learned more French when I was younger so I could keep up with her whispering under her breath. She had wanted us to speak English at home so she could improve, but it meant that French was barely spoken.

"I don't know why you're so opposed to the doctor," Mom said as she walked back into the bathroom with my black silk robe. "Here."

"Thanks," I said, taking the robe and struggling my way into it. The back of the robe got slightly wet from the tiny pool of water I was still sitting in. "As for the doctor, I'd rather crawl my way out of the tub."

"Don't be dramatic," she said as she sat on the closed toilet seat lid. "He's a nice man. Your dad and I like him very much. He shovels our driveway in the winter, and he comes over for Saturday dinner every week. You've been back in town for five weeks, and you still haven't come for a Saturday dinner with us."

"Well, to be fair, I haven't been able to drive myself anywhere in close to a month which means that even if I wanted to come to the dinners, I can't right now."

She sighed. "I don't know why you don't want to come to the dinners. It's a nice tradition. It's the one point of the week when we can sit down together and spend some time talking about our week."

I had been avoiding the dinners because I didn't want to listen to my father rage about my gambling-addicted ex-husband. He still thought that I had made a mistake in not demanding any spousal support, but I didn't want any of my ex's money. Even if he did have any, I didn't think that I would see any of it.

Saturday dinners would just be another chance for my dad to remind me that my life had self-combusted around me, and I wasn't fighting back.

He still couldn't understand that I didn't want to fight. I just wanted to start my life over without the reminder of everything that had gone wrong.

"I'll think about it," I said finally, knowing that I wouldn't give much more thought to it until my ankle was healed.

A knock on the door ended our conversation for the time being as Mom stood to go answer it. Mom would bring it up over and over again until I finally broke down and went to a Saturday dinner. It would probably be better to do it sooner rather than later. That way, she would back off and give me some time to myself.

There were a thousand other things that I needed to get done, including finding a job. I had worked as a kindergarten teacher for the last six years, but when my divorce was finalized three months ago, I left the job I loved and started packing my bags.

With the school year starting this month, I didn't have much hope of finding a job at the local elementary school, but I had applied to the local school board and was waiting to see what came back.

Right now, getting out of the damn bathtub and finding a job was more important than a Saturday dinner.

"Be careful when you go in," Mom said, her voice traveling down the hallway. "Addie's in a bit of a foul mood."

"I wonder why," I said, tying the belt of my robe a little bit tighter. "Maybe it's because you're inviting strange men over to come to see me naked. Hell, why don't we call the fire department in here, too, while we're at it?"

"I see what you mean about the foul mood," Zane said as he stopped at the door and looked down at me with a smile. "Sorry about this."

"It's fine," I said, looking away from him as my cheeks flamed. "I don't think I'm getting out of here any other way."

Zane moved quickly, crossing the bathroom and lifting me out of the tub. He carried me to the living room and set me on the couch.

"How's the ankle feeling?" he asked as he grabbed a bag from beside the door and brought it over. He got down on one knee in front of me and gingerly took my ankle, placing my foot on his knee.

"Like it would be easier to just cut it off at this point," I said, wiggling my toes.

He laughed, his fingers on my skin sending shivers up my body. I considered asking my mother to leave so the doctor and I could get a little closer.

Damn it. You're a grown woman. Get it together.

I was twenty-seven. Being this worked up over an attractive man holding my ankle was ridiculous. It didn't matter that he was looking at me with those pretty green eyes while his dark hair fell in waves across his forehead. He was the kind of handsome that would send girls running straight for him.

"You're going to be at dinner this Saturday, right?" Mom asked as she perched herself on the edge of my coffee table. "We're having steaks on the grill."

"I'll be there," Zane said, shooting her a smile that I swear made my mother swoon. "Do you want me to bring anything?"

Mom looked at me with a smirk. I wanted to lunge off the couch and clamp a hand over her mouth before she could say anything. With my ankle still being inspected, there was nothing I could do to stop her, and she knew it.

"Actually, would you mind bringing Addie? With her ankle the way it is right now, she can't drive, but her dad and I would really like to have her over for dinner."

I scowled at her before looking down at Zane and subtly shaking my head. I could see the hesitation on his face as he weighed his options. When I shook my head again, he grinned and nodded.

"Sure, Fleur. I'll bring her to dinner."

"Excellent," Mom said as she got up and grabbed her purse. "I've got to get going now, but let me know how your ankle is."

She left as if she hadn't just manipulated me into going to the weekly dinner. I stared at the door for a few seconds after she left, trying not to focus on the absence of Zane's touch as he lowered my foot and stood up.

"Your ankle is looking good. You've slightly twisted it again, but after another week or so, you should be good to start running again."

"Are you sure?" I asked, looking down at the ankle. "I don't want to rush into it too soon."

He gave me a flat look, but the corner of his mouth twitched. "If anybody's going to know, it's going to be me."

"Fair enough," I said, standing up and trying to put weight on my ankle.

As I stumbled, he reached out and caught me, helping me balance again. He took a step back, his hands still holding mine as I stood up.

"See?" he said, grinning as I stepped forward. "It's going to hurt again from your fall, but in a week, you should be walking without problem."

"I hope so. I miss running."

"Well, if you want somebody to run or walk with, I'm always looking for some company. You'd have somebody around to help you if you didn't feel comfortable alone with your ankle still weak."

My cheeks flushed a bright red. I hadn't anticipated his offer, and I wasn't sure what to make of it. It was a kind offer, but I didn't know how to spend time with him without telling him how attractive he was. I was sure that it was something he had heard often enough. He didn't need me telling him as well.

And then there was the fact that I didn't want a man in my life yet. My divorce had only been finalized a few months ago after being with my ex-husband, Sam, for five years, married for three years. It didn't seem right to start dating yet.

Dating. All he offered was a running partner. He didn't ask you on a date. Stop getting ahead of yourself.

"Thanks," I said, limping away from him and to the kitchen. "I appreciate it, but I don't think I'm ready for that yet."

I'm not ready to deal with this crush I have on you.

"Take your time. Just remember that you need to keep your ankle moving."

"I will," I said, turning away from him to pour myself a glass of water. I knew that I was being rude, but I didn't want to encourage him to stay any longer.

"Well, I've got to get back to the office. I've got another appointment in half an hour so I should be there on time if I leave now. You're going to be okay by yourself?"

"Yes," I said, limping back over to him and walking with him to the door. "I'll be fine. And about Saturday, you really don't have to come pick me up for dinner."

"Do you think you'll be comfortable driving in three days?" he asked, those bright green eyes giving me a stare I couldn't read.

"No," I said. "Probably not."

"Then I'll pick you up at five on Saturday."

He left, closing the door behind him, and I was left wondering what I had just agreed to. I didn't want to go to a Saturday dinner or spend more time with him, but somehow, I had agreed to both.

I took my glass of water back to the couch and sat down, sipping it and wondering what excuse I could use to get out of an awkward family gathering now.

Chapter 3

Zane

I looked at myself in the mirror, wondering why I was bothering to wear a nice shirt and my cleanest pair of jeans when Addie wasn't planning on being at dinner. She had called me earlier in the day and told me that she wasn't feeling well and was going to call her parents and cancel.

All morning I had been looking forward to seeing her. I thought that it would be a chance to get to know her without her running away from me like she always did.

Her parents had talked about her over the last five years, but I hadn't thought that I would ever meet the woman behind the stories. They said she hated small town life and would never return. When I found Addie in that hole, I realized that the woman my neighbors had been telling stories about was far more interesting than they made her seem.

After running a comb through my hair and still not being satisfied with the way it fell, I gave up.

When my phone started ringing, I groaned and hoped it wasn't Van calling to tell me about another problem someone had cornered him with. Last week he had called me from his brother's hockey game about a woman with a canker sore. I had been in the middle of making dinner, and everything he described over the phone had made my appetite fly out the window.

I loved helping people, but I needed to draw the line

somewhere.

"Hello?"

"Hi," Addie said, her voice soft. "I thought that maybe I would like to go to dinner with the family after all. I've been away for so many years, and I miss them. I know I'm being annoying changing my mind again, but..." She laughed nervously. "Will you please come and pick me up?"

I smiled and grabbed my keys and wallet, tucking them both in my pockets. "I'll be there soon."

"Thank you," she said. "I'll see you when you get here."

"See you soon, Addie."

I was still smiling as I walked to the truck and headed into town. The drive was long, and I might have taken it a little too fast, eager to see Addie. It had been a long time since I had talked to anyone I was this interested in, but something about her drew me in.

Maybe it was the fact that she suggested we invited the fire department to see her nearly naked when Fleur was escorting me in. She had a sense of humor that I found refreshing. She wasn't like the women who ran in my old circle—at least, I didn't think she was, but I wouldn't know until I talked to her more.

When I pulled up outside her apartment, she was standing on the curb. Her auburn hair was hanging in loose curls down her back, blowing with the breeze as she shrank deeper into her denim jacket.

"You look nice," I said as I rounded the front of the truck to help her in. I looked at her black dress and the plain white sneakers she wore. "How's the ankle feeling today?"

"Pretty good," she said as she stepped up into the truck. "It doesn't hurt to walk on it anymore."

"Do you think that you'll be ready to go for that run sometime soon?"

She laughed, her cheeks turning a pretty shade of pink. "Yeah. I think I could be."

"Good. You let me know what day you want to go, and I'll clear my schedule." I glanced over at her as I started the drive to her parents' house. She had an uneasy look on her face as she played with a loose thread on the hem of her dress.

"You don't have to do that for me. I'll be fine."

I chuckled. "Addie, the last time you went running on your own, you fell into an old hunter's trap. I'm going with you, and that's the end of the story."

She sighed and ran her hand through her hair. "I really don't need that."

"And I told you that it's happening," I said, casting another glance her way. "I don't want to see you get hurt again."

Her cheeks turned a darker shade of red. "If you're sure."

"I am. Now, I want to get to know you better. Why did you move back to Blopton?"

Her hands stilled, and her shoulders tensed. I kept my eyes on the road, not saying anything. She would talk when she was ready, and I was not going to push her to say anything before then. The music played softly in the background as she sighed.

"I guess it's going to come out sooner or later since you live beside my parents. Hell, it's probably going to come out tonight."

"You don't have to tell me if you don't want to."

She shook her head. "It's not that. It's just not easy to talk about. My ex-husband, Sam...he was...or is, I really don't know...Sam is addicted to gambling. It took a massive toll on our relationship, and we were broke more often than not. He wouldn't go to treatment, no matter how many times I offered to support him through it. When we lost the house, I decided that I was done."

"That must have been hard."

"It was," she said. "I promised myself that I wouldn't get involved with an addict again."

Her statement had my heart sinking in my chest. My hands tightened on the wheel. If she had sworn off all addicts, we had no hope. Though I was in recovery and had been for four years, I would always be an addict.

Based on what she said, I didn't think she knew about my alcoholism addiction, and it had me wondering if she knew her mother was the one who dragged me to meetings and helped me get clean after I moved to town.

I don't know if I would have gotten through all those long nights without Fleur by my side. I didn't know where I would be without her, but I didn't think I'd still be alive.

I couldn't tell Addie that, though. If she didn't know I was an addict, I didn't want to be the one to break the news to her, even though I knew I had to. That conversation would be difficult. It would draw out all the other demons I had been hiding for so long.

That conversation would rip me to pieces.

It didn't have to be done tonight, though.

As we drove to her parents' house, Addie was more than comfortable carrying on the conversation. She chatted about applying for a teaching job before launching into stories about the children she had taught over the last couple of years.

When we pulled into her parents' driveway, her mom and dad were racing outside before I had even turned the engine off. Addie jumped out of the car and ambled to her parents, hugging them tightly. I sat in the truck for a few minutes longer, letting them have their moment before I went over.

They separated as I walked over to them, tears tracking down Fleur's cheeks. She wiped them away before her daughter could see them, but, at that moment, I saw how hard Addie's divorce had hit all of them.

"What do you say we go inside and start eating? I've been working on a pot roast all day that is going to make your mouths water," Fleur said, linking her arm through her husband's. "Zane, escort Addie to the table, won't you?"

Addie rolled her eyes at her mother's back before leaning into my side to whisper. "You don't have to do that. I can walk myself to the table."

I held out my arm and bowed low, grinning when she laughed. "Your mother is never going to let you walk to the table, so you may as well let me escort you."

"Well, it's hard to argue with that," Addie said as she looped her arm through mine. "Escort away."

I walked with her through the house to the dining room. Fleur enjoyed throwing dinner parties, not just her Saturday night dinners.

"This looks delicious, Mama," Addie said as she looked at the roast on a platter in the center of the table. "Did you make those good little roasted potatoes?"

"Of course," Fleur said as she disappeared into the kitchen before she brought out a tray of potatoes. "The rest of you can sit while I get the water."

"No wine?" Addie asked, her eyebrows furrowing. "When have you ever made a roast without wine?"

Fleur shrugged, purposefully looking away from me. "Your father needs to watch his waistline."

Alex laughed and took his seat, shaking his head. Fleur glanced at me as she left the room, giving me a slight smile. I led Addie to one side of the table before removing my arm from hers and pulling out her chair. She smiled as she sat down.

"Thank you," she said as I pushed into her chair before taking my own beside her.

"Anytime," I said.

Fleur brought the pitcher of water and a few more side dishes to the table before taking her seat. As the food was dished out, she launched into a story from when Addie was a teenager. Addie blushed and laughed, adding her own arguments to the conversation. Alex watched his daughter and wife go back and forth, smiling as he sipped his water.

I couldn't take my eyes off Addie as she laughed with her mother. It was hard to believe that they had spent years apart when they seemed so close.

Addie turned to me, laughing as she grabbed my arm and argued about something her mother had said. I grinned at her, losing myself in her excitement as she spoke. Being around her was simple.

I didn't want to think about how that would change once she found out I was an addict in recovery.

"Are you alright?" Addie whispered later that evening as the dinner dishes were whisked away and dessert was brought out. "You're looking a little green."

"I'm good," I said, looking down at the hand she had placed on my arm. "I'm just a little overwhelmed. You really are a chatterbox when you get going, aren't you?"

She rolled her eyes. "Oh please, you haven't seen anything yet."

I leaned closer to her, lowering my voice so her parents wouldn't hear me. "I'd like to see a hell of a lot more."

Her cheeks flamed as she rolled her eyes away and withdrew her hand. I didn't miss the way her gaze drifted down to my mouth before snapping back up.

"Play your cards right, and you just might," she whispered back before her dessert was placed in front of her.

Her words sent a rush of blood straight from my head to my dick. I cleared my throat and dug into my dessert, ignoring the gleeful look Fleur gave me. Addie snickered beside me before sipping her coffee.

We spent another couple of hours talking to her parents before we left. Addie was smiling from ear to ear as I drove her home.

When I stopped outside her apartment, she leaned across the seat and hugged me tightly. It took me by surprise, but after a second, I wrapped my arms around her and pulled her closer to me. She smelled like an intoxicating blend of vanilla and orange. It was my new favorite smell.

"Thank you for coming to get me tonight," Addie said as she pulled back. "I'll let you know when I plan on going for that run."

"Have a goodnight, Addie," I said, already missing her the moment she was out of my arms.

I sat outside her apartment until I saw her lights come on. When I was sure she was safe, I pulled away from the curb to head home and figure out what I was going to do about my feelings for her.

Chapter 4

Addie

In the last week, I had been restless as my job interview got closer. The kindergarten teacher position came open at the elementary school, and the principal had been very interested in my resume. I had spent the entire week trying to prepare for all the questions he would ask.

I took a deep breath as I pulled down my pencil skirt and adjusted my silk blouse. It was the only outfit I had nice enough and appropriate enough for interviews. I needed to make a good impression. I couldn't keep sitting in my apartment thinking about the doctor who was driving me crazy.

Though I hadn't seen Zane in the week since the dinner at my parents' house, I couldn't get him out of my mind. It didn't help that my mother kept asking about him, even though they lived a few feet from one another. She liked to bring up what she deemed 'our chemistry' at every other turn. It didn't matter that I told her nothing was going on between us. She still had it twisted in her mind that we would be the perfect couple if I wasn't so closed off to love.

It wasn't that I was closed off to love. Some day, I would find somebody to share my life with again. She just didn't understand why I didn't want that time to be right now and with the doctor.

I took one more breath, pushing all thoughts of the overly attractive doctor out of my mind before entering the school.

The office was small and cozy, with a man and woman working the phones. There was a small nurse's office in the back beside the guidance counselor. The principal's office was just beyond that in a small alcove.

"Hello, I'm here for an interview with Principal Rafferty," I said, approaching the man behind the desk with a smile. "Addie Manning."

I changed my name after my divorce, but it still felt weird to say it out loud. It hadn't happened much since the divorce, but it didn't seem to get any easier.

"One moment," he said, disappearing into the little alcove. When he returned, he nodded to me. "This way."

He led me to the principal's office in the back. I stepped inside, and the man behind the desk rose. He held out his hand, and I grasped it, giving it a firm shake before sitting down.

"Addie Manning, correct?" Principal Rafferty asked as he opened my teaching portfolio. "I have to say, I'm impressed."

"Thank you," I said, crossing my legs at the ankles and leaning forward. "I've spent my time trying to build a well-rounded portfolio that properly conveys the passion I have for teaching and helping young people learn."

"What brought you to teaching?"

"I knew I wanted to be a teacher while I was still in middle school. I had some amazing teachers who inspired me and made me believe that I was going to be able to do anything I wanted in the world. I want to be that person for as many children as possible. I believe that they need somebody in their life to believe in them, especially if they aren't getting that in their home lives."

Principal Rafferty nodded and flipped to another section of my portfolio. "I see that you put a focus on reading and writing. It's more of a focus than we tend to put on it here."

"Being able to read and write are the foundations of school. While I still teach the curriculum for science and math, I make sure reading and writing are largely incorporated into those subjects."

He nodded again. "Very good. I have to be honest...this interview is going to be very short. I need a teacher, and you're highly qualified. When I called your references, they all had wonderful things to say about you and had been heartbroken when you moved away. Since school is in session, there's already a classroom set up for you."

"Am I allowed to come in on a weekend and redo it?" I asked.

"Absolutely. Do whatever you want with the classroom as long as it falls within fire code." He shut my portfolio and pushed it to the side. "What do you say we go get you some contracts to read over and give you a tour of the school?"

"I can't wait."

***

When I got home, I was feeling better than I had in weeks. It felt like I was finally starting to build a life for myself after a couple of months of not knowing who I was or where I was going. Now, I had a job and was starting to settle down in the town that raised me. Everything felt like it was slowly starting to fall back into place.

I changed out of my interview outfit and pulled on a pair of shorts and a sports bra. I grabbed a sweater and my sneakers, lacing them up before heading out the door.

Stretching out, my muscles felt better than they had in weeks. The autumn air was crisp and fresh as the leaves fell to the ground. I pulled my hair up into a high ponytail, sliding the elastic off my wrist to tie it up. After taking a deep breath, I ran around the back of my apartment to the trail that began there.

My footsteps were steady and sure as I hit the trail. It didn't take long for the pain to start creeping back into my ankle. I slowed to a walk, taking my time to stretch and roll my ankle. The pain disappeared after a few minutes, and I started running again.

"Shit," I said as I slowed down again. There was a dull

throbbing in my ankle that wouldn't go away.

For the next few minutes, I rotated between jogging and walking, trying to move like I wasn't in pain. Finally, I had to admit defeat. I sat down on a nearby bench and kicked off my shoe, trying to massage the pain out of my ankle.

Once I was sure that I could start running again, I put my shoe on and took off running. I didn't make it very far, needing to lean against a tree when the pain nearly leveled me to the ground.

"You were supposed to call me when you were ready to go running again."

I looked to my right and saw Zane at the top of a small hill. He jogged down it and stopped beside me, kneeling on the ground.

"Give me your foot."

"I'm fine. It's just a little bit of pain. Nothing that I can't handle."

"Addie, give me your damn foot and stop pretending that you don't need somebody to help you."

I lifted my foot and put it on his knee. Zane took off the shoe and started running his fingers along my ankle. Shivers ran up my spine at the feeling of his hands on my body again. I shoved the shivers away, reminding myself that he was a medical professional looking at my injury.

"It's swollen again. Did you twist it at all while running?"

"No," I said as he helped me put my shoe back on but tied it looser. "I was running, but I stretched first. I didn't think that there was anything wrong."

"You should have called me before you went out running. I would have met you and been able to help you sooner."

"Don't lecture me," I said as he stood up and dusted the dirt off his clothing. "I don't need you to always come to my rescue."

He scoffed and picked me up, tossing me over his shoulder. "From this angle, it looks like you do."

"What the hell do you think you're doing?" I asked, staring at his ass.

"Since you won't cooperate, we're doing things my way."

I glared at his back, hating how attractive I found him at that moment, even though I wasn't a fan of being manhandled back to my apartment.

"Who said I wouldn't cooperate?"

He chuckled. "I don't think you've ever cooperated with anyone a day in your life."

"I resent that."

"But am I wrong?" he asked, shifting me slightly as he neared my apartment building. At my silence, he laughed. "I didn't think so."

"You can't just go around carrying people and acting like you can tell them what to do."

Zane hummed. "Actually, I'm a doctor. It's kind of in my job description."

"Apparently so is a god complex."

Zane laughed and put me on the ground as he stopped outside my building. "You need to alternate ice and heat on that ankle. Next time you decide to go for a run, call me first."

"Fine," I said, crossing my arms and glaring at him, trying to fight the smile that threatened to spread across my face.

After so long being the person that cared for others, it was nice to have someone looking out for me.

"I'm going to go shower and then get straight to that heat and ice," I said, pulling my key out of my bra. Zane's gaze darted to his chest before he gave me that heated stare.

"Do you want someone there in case you fall again?" he asked, his tone teasing despite the heat in his eyes.

"Fine, but you keep your hands to yourself, and your ass planted on my couch. This isn't a free show."

He laughed and followed me inside the building. "I'll be sitting on the couch and keeping my eyes to myself."

I rolled my eyes at him before disappearing into my bathroom. If I was being honest, it was nice to know he was sitting out there waiting to help me in case I did fall again. I wasn't sure that my ankle wouldn't give out while I was showering. Even now, while limping on it, I felt like I was going to fall down.

Once showered and dressed, I walked back into the living room to find Zane scrolling through his phone. He looked up when I entered the room, smiling.

"How's the ankle feel?" he asked.

"Not great," I said, sitting on the couch beside him. He reached down and pulled my foot into his lap, massaging my sore ankle. "That feels amazing."

He chuckled and pressed his thumbs harder into my skin. "See what happens when you let people help you?"

"Nobody likes a know-it-all," I said, wiggling my toes at him. My stomach growled, and I was reminded that I hadn't had food since breakfast. "How about I order a pizza, and you stay to have a slice or two since you've saved me twice now?"

He gave me a smile that had my heart skipping a beat. "I would like that very much."

I got up and ordered the pizza before sitting back down with him. Zane said nothing as he started massaging my ankle again while I turned on a movie. By the time the pizza arrived, my ankle was feeling a million times better, and my entire body was on fire.

"So," I said as I pulled a slice out of the box and nearly burned my mouth on the hot cheese. "Why come to run a solo practice in a small town?"

Zane sighed as he grabbed his own slice and shrugged. "A lot of horrible things have happened in my life, and after a while, I got tired of having reminders everywhere. Moving out here seemed like the right choice. I was away from the reminders, and I got to slow down."

"What's it like being a doctor?" I asked, getting the sense that he didn't want to talk about the demons of his past.

"I love it. I love being able to help people. I never thought when I was younger that it's what I'd do, but once I started medical school, I couldn't think of doing anything else."

Zane's hands moved quickly as he talked about being a doctor. I could see the passion on his face as he spoke. The more he talked, the more I was sucked in. I don't know how long we talked, but by the time he left, the stars were out, and the moon shone bright.

For the first time in a long time, I slept through the night and dreamed of the future.

Chapter 5

Zane

The last person I thought I'd see when I walked out of my Alcoholics Anonymous meeting a few days later was Addie. Yet, there she was across the street with groceries balanced on her hips. She shuffled the bags, stumbling slightly as she walked across the uneven sidewalk.

I ducked my head and crossed the street, pretending like I hadn't just come from an addiction meeting. While I knew that I needed help and wanted others to get help when they needed it, I didn't want her to know about my struggles yet. She had said that she would never get involved with an addict again. Addie had made that very clear, and I wasn't sure how to tell her. I didn't want to ruin my chances with her.

How do you think it's going to go when she finds out you lied to her? the nasty voice in the back of my head asked.

"Hey, Addie," I said, emerging from the opposite side of where the meeting was held. I took long strides until I was at her side. I took the bags from her. "The sidewalk is shit, and with your ankle still hurting, you're only going to make it worse."

"I thought I told you that I could take care of myself," she said, reaching for the bags.

I held them out of her reach with a smile. "I know you can. It's just not a good idea to be walking home on that ankle with all these groceries."

Addie rolled her eyes as though she was smiling. "I guess you're right."

"Can you repeat that? Or maybe write it down? It could be the first and only time you ever say it."

Addie laughed, and the sound was music to my ears. She led the way down Main Street, heading toward her apartment. As we walked, she told me about her lesson plans for her new students. She was nearly bouncing as she turned to tell me everything she planned to do on her first day at school.

"Alright," she said, turning to me as we reached her apartment a few minutes later. "Tell me what's new at the clinic."

"I'm thinking of repainting, and somehow Van invited himself over for dinner tonight."

Addie laughed. "When I first came to the clinic, I couldn't remember him, but it came back to me slowly. He's a character that one. I remember him when he was younger. He didn't care if people wanted him around or not. He was always determined to be exactly where he wanted to be, and nobody could change his mind."

"Good to know that nothing has ever changed with him, then."

She gave me that stunning smile again. "You're going to have a great dinner, even if he is years younger than you."

I looked at her, knowing from her patient file that she was a few years younger than me. "Age is just a number. Van's a good kid, and I think he'll go far in life."

"He's always done everything that he puts his mind to, so I don't doubt it." She glanced down at her watch. "I should let you get going then."

"Addie, do you want to join us?"

Addie shook her head and took the bags from me. "Thanks for the offer, but I'd hate to ruin your night."

"You wouldn't be ruining it," I said.

"I would. Have a good time, Zane. Maybe we could go out for that run sometime soon?"

"Just tell me the time and what trail," I said.

Addie nodded and went inside. I stood outside and stared at the door for a minute before beginning my walk back to the grocery store. With Van coming over, I needed something to make for dinner, and I suspected that I would need a lot of it. After seeing what he packed for himself for lunch, I didn't think a burger and a fistful of chips was going to cut it.

I was going to need to start keeping more food in my house, especially if people started coming over more. If Addie came over, I didn't want to look like that adult who couldn't take care of himself and lived off a bottle of ketchup, cheese, and something questionable in the back of the fridge.

With that in mind, I headed into the grocery store with no clue what to make for dinner tonight.

***

"So," Van said as he took another hot dog off the grill. "You've been spending a lot of time around town with Addie."

"How do you even know that?" I asked, nearly choking on my drink.

"After five years you still have no clue how gossip spreads in this town." Van grinned and put more mustard on his hot dog than any human should. "That's cute. I heard it at the barbershop. One of the guys there heard it from his wife."

"And who else knows about the amount of time I've been spending around Addie?"

Van shrugged. "Most of town. Fleur's giddy about it."

I groaned and ran a hand down my face. "Perfect."

"Don't worry," Van said, a shit-eating grin on his face. "Nobody has started talking about the wedding yet, but I suspect that it's only a matter of time."

I rolled my eyes and took a long sip of my drink. "We're not even dating. Don't get ahead of yourself."

"You want to date her, though, which means that there's hope for a marriage. Do I get to be your best man?"

Van's grin was infectious, even as I sighed. I had a few friends in town, but even after years of living among the locals, Van was my closest friend. If I did have a wedding, he would be the best man without a doubt.

"You drive me insane," I said, not bothering to answer him. "I'm not getting married anytime soon."

"Because you haven't even asked Addie yet."

"What makes you think I'm going to ask Addie?"

Van shrugged. "I don't know. Why do you keep trying to lie to yourself?"

"I'm not lying to myself at all. I know how I feel about her but with my alcoholism, getting involved with her is a bad idea. She doesn't want to have anything to do with addicts."

"You're in recovery," Van said. "You're in recovery and have been in recovery for a few years. You work hard to stay sober, and to be honest, I don't know how you do it with all that you've been through."

"It's not easy," I said. "It takes a lot of work, and there're days when I still feel like drinking, so I don't have to think about everything that happened."

"I think if you're honest with Addie about it, she'll have all the information she needs to make a decision. Who knows, she might just surprise you."

I sighed and ran a hand through my hair. I would tell her the truth one day; I just didn't know when that day would be.

"Why don't you just go over there and tell her how you feel? I've been watching you stare after her for weeks, and honestly, it's getting to the point where you either need to do something about it or let it go."

He was right, and I knew he was right. Sitting around and pining after she wasn't doing me any good. Van made it sound easier than it was. He made it sound like she would find out about the skeletons I kept buried deep in my closet and would not care.

That she would accept me for who I was.

Alcoholism was just the beginning, though. I couldn't imagine anyone who would look past all the other things I had done.

"You look like you're starting to spiral," Van said as I grabbed another bottle of water from the cooler I had brought outside earlier in the evening. "Stop looking like you're spiraling. It's going to be fine."

"I'm a grown man. It shouldn't be this hard."

"You're a grown man who doesn't believe he's worthy of love due to a couple of mistakes he made in his life." Van smirked and leaned back in his chair. "One of those TV doctors taught me that."

I laughed and shook my head, the tension of the conversation easing. As he got another hot dog, Van grinned and settled back in his chair with the bottle of mustard.

"I'm serious. You want her. Go get her. Stop acting like she's going to turn you away when she doesn't even know the truth."

"You're acting like it's your job to get us together."

"She likes you. You like her. I don't see the problem. If you need to send her one of those check yes or no love notes, I'm excellent at drawing boxes."

I rolled my eyes at him, my lips twitching. If I smiled again, it would only encourage him to keep talking. Instead, I got up, turned off the grill, and closed the lid to keep the last few hot dogs warm. I had no doubt that Van would finish them off before he left. He seemed to have a hollow leg.

"All I'm saying is that you don't want to wait until it's too late. Now that her ankle's better and she's going out, somebody else is going to notice her."

I scowled at him. "Why do you keep trying to get me worked up?"

Van shrugged. "Why do you keep letting it work? You're the one that's interested in her. Do something about it."

"Fine," I said, getting up and heading for the house. "Lock up before you leave. You know where the spare key is."

"Where are you going?" Van called after me, sounding amused.

"You said I should do something about it," I said, looking over my shoulder at him. "So, I'm going to go do something about it."

***

During the drive to Addie's house, I nearly talked myself into turning around and driving home half a dozen times. Van would be waiting until I got back, even though I told him to lock up when he left. There was no way he would go home before he knew what had happened.

Having to admit that I was a coward was the only reason I didn't back out and left talking to Addie for another day. Of course, I didn't know when that other day would come.

I parked along the curb beside her apartment and drummed my fingers on the wheel.

The worst that can happen is that she already knows about the alcoholism and wants nothing to do with you.

I pushed the thought as far away from me as I could and got out of the truck. With a deep breath, I walked to her door and rang the bell, hoping that she was home.

Addie opened the door with a grin. "What are you doing here? I thought you had that dinner with Van tonight."

"I did," I said, swallowing hard as my heart hammered in my chest. "But there's been something on my mind lately."

Addie raised an eyebrow and crossed her arms as she leaned against the doorframe. "You came all the way over here to tell me that you couldn't get something out of your mind?"

"No. I came over here to tell you that I can't get you out of my head since we met a couple of weeks ago."

She gave me a blinding smile, and what little resolve and hesitation I had left faded into the background. I closed the distance between us as she reached for me. As my arms went around her, her mouth slanted against mine. The kiss was soft and sweet, and when she pulled away, I wanted to pull her back.

"Well," she said as she looked at me, her cheeks flushed and her eyes bright. "I just opened a bottle of wine. Do you want to come in and have a drink?"

"Do you have coffee? It's been a long day, and I could use a hot drink."

She stepped aside and held the door open. "Do I have coffee? Zane, I love coffee more than I love most things in life."

I followed her inside, all thoughts of telling her about my addiction gone as I tried to figure out where I would take her on our first date.

Chapter 6

Addie

Zane and I spent most evenings together after work for the last two weeks. There was nothing more relaxing than coming home from being mauled by kindergarteners all day long and having Zane show up with groceries to make dinner. Most of the time, he sat on the couch and entertained me while I ate dinner.

It had only taken him one attempt at making burgers for dinner for me to decide that I would do the cooking when we ate in. I wasn't risking food poisoning or eating a brick of charcoal.

And then there were the morning runs. Zane knew all the new trails in town and was more than happy to wake up before the sun and run with me. Every morning he picked me up with coffee in hand and drove me to a trailhead. This morning was no exception.

When I left my apartment, he was already sitting in his truck. As soon as I got in, he handed me a coffee and grinned.

"Rough morning?" he asked, playing with the end of my ponytail.

"How could you tell?" I asked.

"You look like you didn't sleep at all."

"That's a nice way of saying I look like shit," I said, my tone teasing. I took a long sip of coffee, moaning when the coffee hit my tired soul. "This is the best coffee yet."

"You say that every morning," he said, his hand resting on my thigh as he drove out of town. His fingers drifted along my thigh, lighting a fire wherever he touched.

"You keep doing that, and we're going to have a problem," I said, looking pointedly down at his hand.

Zane laughed and squeezed my thigh, his hand drifting higher before he put both hands on the wheel. "That better?"

"Nope."

"Good."

It didn't take long to reach the trailhead. We ran together until the sun came up before turning and heading back to the truck. Running always left me feeling better than when I woke up.

"I haven't seen your house yet," I said as we got back in the truck. "It's closer to here than my place, and I'm starving."

Zane chuckled. "Inviting yourself over for breakfast?"

I shrugged and leaned back in my seat, sipping what was left of my cold coffee. His laughter made my heart skip a beat. It had been a long time since a man made me feel the way that he did. How he looked at me sent liquid heat flooding my body to my core. It had only been nearly two months, but I wanted him more than I had ever wanted anybody else.

Zane turned up the music as he drove to his house. When we reached his driveway, I turned my face away from the window, hoping my mother wasn't outside. I didn't want her to see me and start getting all kinds of ideas in her head, especially when the relationship was so new.

"I think we're in the clear," Zane said, amusement in his voice as he parked the truck. "Your mom is out front, and your dad's car is gone, so I doubt he's home. If we make a run for the back door, Fleur won't see you."

I blushed and looked over at him. "I just don't want her to get excited until we know where this is going, and we've been together a bit longer."

He nodded and opened his door. "I understand. Now come on, I bet I can beat you to the back door."

"You're on," I said with a grin as I got out.

He took off running before I even reached the front of the truck. I smothered my laughter, not wanting my mom to hear me, and followed after him. Even though I knew I wasn't going to beat him, I still tried. When we got to his back porch, he grabbed me around the waist and tossed me over his shoulder.

I was laughing as he walked into the house and tossed me onto the couch. Zane was quick to follow, hovering over me as we kissed. My fingers threaded through his hair as he leaned into me. I pulled him closer, his tongue tangling with mine as I hooked a leg around his hip.

Zane pulled back and looked down at me, heat in his eyes. "As much as I want to continue this, I'm sweaty and gross from running."

"Your point?" I asked, both legs around his waist.

"We're going for a shower."

"Sounds good to me."

Zane chuckled and wrapped his arms around me, lifting me from the couch and walking with me down the hall, his mouth trailing up and down my neck. I moaned as he held me up against a wall, pulling my shirt off and tossing it to one side.

His hands massaged my breasts, pulling my bra out of the way before he dipped his head to suck a nipple into his mouth. I moaned, writhing against his hardened length and trying to relieve some of the tension building between my legs.

We reached the bathroom, and Zane set me on the counter. I watched him as he stripped out of his clothes before turning on the massive shower. The walls of the shower were made entirely of glass, and there was more than enough room for two people inside. Steam fogged up the glass almost immediately.

I hopped down from the counter and stripped out of my clothes, tossing my hair tie on the counter before stepping into the shower with an added sway to my hips. I heard Zane's groan moments before he followed me into the shower, his chest against my back as his hands ran up my body.

Zane toyed with my nipples as the hot water hit my skin. I moaned, leaning back into him as one of his hands drifted down my stomach. His fingers found my clit, circling it slowly and driving me insane.

"Faster," I said breathlessly as he nipped and sucked at my neck.

"You want more?" he asked, his voice raspy as he withdrew his hand. "Not yet."

He spun me around and got on his knees, lifting one of my legs over his shoulder. Zane pressed one finger slowly inside me while he flattened his tongue against my clit. I moaned as he swirled his tongue at the same time he started thrusting his finger faster.

"Yes," I moaned, leaning back against the wall. My fingers threaded through his hair as my inner walls clenched around him. I ground against him, aching for relief as he added another finger.

When he hooked his fingers, rocking them harder, I came apart around him.

"Yes, baby," he said, still rocking his fingers as the last of my orgasm flooded through me. He stood up and claimed my mouth in a scorching kiss when I finally stopped shuddering.

He stepped out of the shower for a moment before he came back, sliding a condom down his cock. My tongue darted out, licking my lower lip before he kissed me again. I hooked one of my legs around his hip, leaning back against the glass. Water rained down over us as he slipped inside me. My inner walls clenched around him as he took a nipple in his mouth, sucking hard as he thrust deeper inside of me. I moaned, rocking my hips in time with his thrusts.

Zane wrapped my hair around his hand, pulling my head back. With the other, he held the soft flesh around my waist. I arched my back, the angle shifting as he thrust harder. His fingers dropped to my hips, gripping the soft flesh so hard I knew I was going to have bruises later on. The thought of his marks on my body only made my orgasm come that much harder.

"Fuck, that feels good," he said, giving one final thrust before he fell apart. He grinned as he looked down at me. "I don't know how I'm going to look your father in the eye after that."

"Good thing we have all day before Saturday dinner. We can give you some more reasons not to look him in the eye."

Zane laughed and grabbed the soap, motioning for me to turn around. "Sounds good to me."

***

When we walked into my parents' house, Zane and I were back to being friends and nothing more—at least until we could get back to his house later that evening. It was hard to pretend that I didn't want to drag him into a room and have my way with him again.

"Stop looking at me like you've seen me naked," I hissed when my parents left the room to start bringing the food in.

"That's because I have," he said under his breath.

My cheeks felt like they were on fire as my parents walked back into the room carrying platters of food. I reached for my water and took a long sip, squeezing my thighs together.

I was thankful I was wearing underwear—even when Zane suggested I shouldn't—but I didn't think they were going to survive beyond dinner. Not with how he was looking at me and rubbed my thigh beneath the table.

Grabbing his hand, I shoved it off my leg. I needed to focus on not being a couple, especially with my mom glancing between us like she knew something was happening. It wouldn't surprise me if she did.

"So," Mom asked, her gaze still darting between us as I scooped stew into my bowl. "Is there anything new and exciting going on in your life?"

Zane saved me from having to lie to her more by launching into a story about one of the patients from the clinic. Dad laughed and joked with him while I kept avoiding glances from my mom.

After dinner, I was sure that she was going to pull me to the side and demand to know what was going on, but she didn't. She stopped looking at us during dessert, a smirk on her face. My heart was hammering as I wondered how much she had pieced together.

"You know," Mom said as she walked into the living room carrying a tray with cups of coffee. "You two would make a cute couple. You look good together."

It was at that moment that I knew she had figured it out. I had never been good at keeping secrets from her. My cheeks flamed as I took a cup of coffee. I stared down at it, avoiding the way her gaze lingered on me before she moved on.

"Addie doesn't need to find anyone else yet," Dad said before sipping on his coffee. "Not after that last idiot she was with. I'd still like to bury him so deep they'll never find him."

"Dad, that's unnecessary," I said, wishing that the ground would open me up and swallow me whole. "That part of my life is over, and I'll start dating again whenever I feel ready."

Mom chuckled as she took her seat. "And who might that lucky man be?"

"I don't know. I didn't say that I was ready to date yet."

Mom smirked, humming as she leaned back in her chair. Zane stepped in and started talking with my dad about football, but the damage was already done. If Mom wasn't sure before, she was now.

There would be no more denying it the next time I was over, but for now, I was going to live in my ignorant bliss and pretend that nothing had happened. I wanted to keep the relationship to myself for a little while longer.

Chapter 7

Zane

The dozen tables that occupied the bar were filled with people watching sports. It was a typical night at the bar, and I only knew that because I had been sitting at the bar for the last four nights after I left Addie's house.

It's been almost six years since I lost my first patient, and the pain hasn't eased. I lost two years of my life to alcoholism after that death. Other doctors had said that time would make it easier, but it didn't.

What was supposed to have been a routine appendix removal for a child went wrong. Even now, what happened in that operating room still haunted my dreams. The appendix burst after we had barely gotten the little girl on the table open. Toxins spilled into her body before I knew what was happening.

I couldn't save her. I had to call time of death and then tell her parents that it was my fault their daughter had died. I hadn't been fast enough. I hadn't gotten to her in time. I hadn't known what to do to save her.

Her blood was on my hands, and no matter how many times I tried to wash them clean, I couldn't.

"Do you want anything to drink?" the bartender asked, approaching me and breaking me out of my spiral.

"Water, please," I said though I was craving something a lot stronger than water.

It was near the anniversary when I considered drinking the most. The memories of that day came flooding back to me as if they were happening in real-time. The mother's screams still echoed in my ears each time I had to tell a patient bad news.

That one loss had been enough to make me give up surgery forever. That, and after the Chief of General Surgery found out about my drinking problem, I was told that I could either quit and move on, or I could be fired and ruin my life. The day I was given the ultimatum, I had been sober enough to make a smart decision.

"Are you sure you don't want something else?" the bartender asked, looking at the still-full glass of water in my hand nearly a half an hour later.

I looked at the bottles lining the back wall, my hand clenched tight around my glass. For a moment, I was worried it was going to break. I released my grip and shook my head.

"Water's fine. Thanks."

"Anything to eat then? Kitchen's still open for a few more hours."

My stomach growled, and it was only then that I realized I hadn't eaten anything since yesterday. "Maybe a burger."

He nodded and walked to the register. "Maybe a burger coming up."

I drummed my fingers on the table, glancing up every now and then at the football game on the TV. I had no clue what was happening—football was never a sport I followed, but it was better than staring at the bottles in the back row.

"I didn't know you'd be here."

My spine stiffened at the sound of Addie's voice. When I had left her apartment earlier, she said that she was going out with a few of the other teachers from school. I hadn't expected her to come here. The bar was a bit of a dive, but there was another one in town that had live music and a better atmosphere.

If I had thought that she would have come to this bar, I would have gone to the other one to wallow in my misery.

I plastered on a grin and turned to face her. "Hey, I didn't know you guys would be coming here."

She wrapped me in a tight hug and kissed my cheek before wiping away the lipstick stain. "Yeah. One of the girls said she likes the food here better. Do you want to join us?"

"Nope," I said, grinning at her. "You have your night with your friends. I'm just picking up some food to go so I don't have to go hungry at home."

She stared at me for a moment, and her smile turned into a frown. "Are you okay?"

"I'm fine. It's just been a long day."

Her eyebrows pulled closer together, a fine line appearing between them. "Okay. If you're sure, you're okay."

"I'm sure. Go have fun, and I'll see you later."

She grinned again, and I kissed her before she disappeared into the crowd to join her friends. As soon as she was gone, I flagged the bartender down and asked him to make my burger to-go.

***

I drove around for hours, not wanting to go home but not sure where else I could go. Fleur had made it clear that I needed to come over whenever I was struggling, but it was late, and I was sure she was asleep.

When I finally got home, Addie was sitting on my front porch with the blanket she kept in the back of her car wrapped around her shoulders. She was looking down at the phone in her hands, as if she was ready to throw it across the yard.

"Hey," I said as I got out of the truck and crossed the yard. "I didn't think you'd be coming over tonight."

She looked up at me with red-rimmed eyes and clutched the phone tighter. "What are you lying to me about?"

My heart stopped in my chest. A million different lies and excuses flashed through my mind. I should have told her before

45

now. I could have told her dozens of times leading up to now.

"And don't try to tell me that you're not lying about anything. I'm not going to be putting up with another man lying to me, so if you have something to come clean about, you better do it now."

I wanted to ask her what would happen if I didn't, but I already knew based on the look on her face. If I didn't tell her what was going on in my life, she would walk out of it forever.

Hell, she still might, even after I told her everything.

It was a risk that I had to take.

"I'm struggling," I said as I sat down beside her. The words nearly got caught in my throat. It wasn't the first time I had said them, but they still felt nearly impossible to say.

"Struggling with what?"

"A lot of things. Alcoholism being the worst one."

She froze beside me, her shoulders tensing as she looked at me. The hurt in her eyes nearly tore me in half.

"I should have told you about it before I ever kissed you. I know I should have. I was a coward. I thought you would never give me a chance if you knew I'm an addict."

"I've never seen you drink," she says, her words sounding choked as if there's a lump caught in her throat.

"I'm in recovery. Have been for the last four years. Still an addict, though."

She nodded, her phone dropping into her lap before she ran her hands down her face. "So, you're struggling."

"Tomorrow is the anniversary of the death of one of my patients during surgery."

"You're not a surgeon," Addie said, clutching the blanket tighter around her body. She held onto it as if it was the only thing keeping her afloat. "How could you kill a patient?"

"I was a general surgeon. A little girl came in with pain near her appendix. We knew that it was about to burst, but the hospital was busy that night. The trauma surgeons were busy, the emergency room was packed, and I overlooked her for a long time."

I paused and blinked away the tears in my eyes. It felt like my chest was closing in on itself as I looked away from her.

"By the time we got to the operating room and got her open, it was too late. Toxins were spilling into her body, and there was nothing that we could do to save her."

"I'm so sorry," Addie said, reaching for my hand. She laced her fingers through mine and squeezed it tight.

"After I told her parents that I killed their daughter, I started drinking. Heavily. It only got worse until I was told that I could either quit or be fired. I quit and kept drinking. I moved here after a year of drinking and took another year to get clean."

"And now the anniversary date has brought it all back." Addie ran her hand through her hair. "You should have told me about this."

"I was scared that you were going to want nothing to do with me if you knew I was an addict. You made it pretty clear that you wanted nothing to do with addicts ever again."

She sighed and squeezed my hand again before dropping it. "You still should have told me. That was my decision to make, not yours."

"And you can still make whatever decision you want," I said, shuffling a few inches away from her. The physical distance between us didn't make me feel any better, but if she was going to walk away, she could.

"Are you sober now?"

"I don't want to be," I said, hating the truth. I wanted to drink. I wanted to lose myself in the alcohol and numb all the pain for the next few days. "But yes. I haven't had a drink in the last four years."

Those few days would turn into a few weeks, which would turn into a few months. Hell, it could turn into a few years. I wanted to lose myself, but I couldn't. I didn't know if I would ever find myself again.

"Call your sponsor," she said as she stood up. "I'm going to go borrow a shirt and go put on a movie. If you want to talk after, I'll be there."

"You're not leaving?" I asked, feeling hope for the first time when thinking about her and my addiction.

Addie shook her head. "I'm disappointed that you hid that from me, especially knowing what I've been through, but it's your problem to share."

"You're not leaving then?" I asked again, needing to make sure that this wasn't a dream.

"I'm not leaving." She bent down and kissed my cheek. "I'm not leaving you to deal with this alone. Just don't ever lie to me again."

"I won't."

"Thank you."

Even as she spoke, I could hear the lump that was caught in her throat. I hoped that she would be okay on her own for a few hours, but she was right. I needed to call my sponsor and talk about everything going through my head. I needed someone who understood what it was like to talk me down from the ledge.

I watched her go inside and waited until I knew she was nowhere near the door before I pulled out my phone and called Fleur.

Chapter 8

Addie

When I woke up the next morning, it felt like I had been hit by a truck. The sleep I had gotten the night before was fitful at best. Everything that Zane told me while we were sitting on his porch kept running through my mind.

He was an addict. He had kept that from me. I had no right to be angry—we had just started dating a few weeks ago—but I was. I was so angry that he didn't tell me when he knew what had happened with my ex-husband.

I looked at him as he slept beside me and wondered if I would have done anything differently if he had told me months ago. He was snoring, rolling over onto his side. I looked at the peaceful expression on his face and knew that if he had told me before we started dating, I wouldn't have even entertained a date.

I never would've given him a chance.

As he slept, I slid out of bed and made my way to the living room. I needed a few minutes by myself before he woke up to think about what I was going to do.

Last night, I told him that I wasn't going to let him go through this alone, and I wasn't. I refused to let him suffer alone, but it was hard. Each time I thought about his addiction, I thought about my ex-husband's addiction.

Unlike Sam, Zane was working on keeping himself clean. He was working on avoiding his addiction, and he was looking for help. He didn't want to live in his addiction. He had known that there was something wrong, and he got help.

I kept reminding myself of that as I walked out to my car and got the bag of clothing from the back.

After I got changed, I started stretching. A run was what I needed to clear my head. I needed to get some fresh air, and hopefully, the chilly air would be enough to shock my system.

"Going for a run?" Zane asked as he walked into the living room.

"Yeah. You coming?"

The words sounded hollow even to me. I wanted him to come with me and pretend that everything was normal, even if it was for a short time. When we got back from the run, we were going to have some talking to do.

"Yeah, just let me get changed," he said before disappearing back into the bedroom.

When he came out, we didn't say anything to each other. I didn't know what I could say to him at that moment. If we were running, it would be easier to pretend that nothing was wrong.

Sitting in the truck next to each other as he drove us to our favorite trailhead was tense and awkward. There was more left unsaid between us that still needed to come out. There was hurt on both sides, and neither of us knew what to say.

"You know, I started running when the urge to drink was bad." Zane sighed and drummed his fingers on the wheel. "It was the only thing that could force me to have a clear head. Mainly because I was so out of shape that running hurt."

"Is that still why you run?"

"No. It just became a habit. After that, I started to enjoy running."

"Well, at least you found something that worked for you," I said. I cringed when I heard how it came out, but nothing else could be said.

We fell silent again as he drove farther away from town. Zane sighed and rolled the window down, letting the cold air into the car before he turned the radio up. I was glad for the distraction.

When we got to the trailhead, we stretched before we took off running. The weight that had been placed on my shoulders over the last day started to lift. Every ounce of panic that I had been feeling started to fade away. I wanted to do something fun. I wanted to have fun before we had to go back and start dealing with the ocean of shit we'd have to wade through.

"You're it," I said, tapping Zane on the shoulder before taking a sharp turn and running in the opposite direction.

I heard Zane's laugh far behind me as I ran as fast as I could. I knew it was only a matter of time before he caught me, but I was going to give him one hell of a chase before then.

As I heard him approaching, I ducked behind one of the trees. He ran by, calling my name as I kept myself hidden from him. I thought he had disappeared until arms wrapped around my waist and hauled me back against a hard body.

"You're it," he said, his voice husky in my ear. I could feel his erection pressing against my ample backside as his lips trailed up and down my neck.

As our clothes started falling off, I only grew more excited. We were only a few feet from the trail. Anybody could walk by and see us at any moment.

"Mmm, you're wet," he said as his fingers circled my clit before dipping inside me.

I moaned, writhing against his hand as he pushed me back against a tree. The bark was rough as it bit into my back, the pain bringing more pleasure.

"Fuck," he groaned. "I didn't bring anything."

"I've got an IUD, and I'm clean."

His clothes were off as soon as the words were out of my mouth.

"I'm clean, too," he said.

I embraced him before kissing my way down his body until I

was on my knees in front of him. The rocks and sticks dug into my knees, sending another shiver of pleasure up my spine.

I gripped his cock, smoothing my thumb over the silky head before I licked my way down his shaft. His hands knotted in my hair when I licked my way back up the other side. His eyes rolled back as I took his cock in my mouth, flattening my tongue against the underside as I took him as deep as possible.

He moaned as I sucked his cock, working the head with my tongue. His hips moved in time with my sucking, pushing himself deeper and deeper. When I felt him tensing, he pulled back.

"Get up, turn around, and bend over."

Heat pooled between my legs as I did what he said, bracing myself against a log. He entered me from behind in one swift move. As he was thrusting, he reached around my body, tweaking my nipples as he pulled me upright against him. I moaned as my inner walls squeezed him, my hand drifting down to my clit.

I rubbed my clit as he was thrusting. His hands traced heat down my body, swirling softly along the soft pooch of my belly, waist, across my hips before moving up to my breasts, massaging them. When my walls started clamping down on him again, he stopped playing with my nipples and clamped a hand over my mouth.

"You wouldn't want anyone to hear you scream my name while I'm fucking you," he whispered, nipping at my earlobe. "Or come see the way you're touching yourself while I'm buried inside you."

His words were all it took to send me over the edge, screaming his name against his hand. He thrust faster, groaning as he finished.

We stepped away from each other, panting and searching for our clothes. Once I was dressed, I wrapped my arms around him.

"We should probably go get cleaned up," Zane said, kissing my forehead.

"Let's go home."

***

After a shower that turned into another round of sex and avoiding the discussion we needed to have, I walked into the kitchen to make a cup of coffee. Zane was still in the shower, singing along with a song I didn't know.

When I opened the cupboard where he normally kept the coffee, it wasn't there. I sighed and looked around the kitchen, wondering where he would have put it. Not once in the time that I had been dating him had he ever put groceries away in the same spot twice. It seemed like he thrived on the chaos.

After opening a few of the cabinets, I was getting ready to drive into town to just pick up the coffee. Searching for the grinds was becoming an endless failure. I opened another cupboard and felt the world fall out from beneath me.

Zane came whistling into the kitchen, but the whistling cut out when I turned around with a bottle of bourbon and a glass in my hand. There was a splash of liquid still left in the glass that stank of bourbon. Behind that bottle, there had been three other empty ones. He had downed three other bottles in an effort to numb the pain, and I had been blind to all of it.

I felt like such an idiot.

I kept falling for men who lied to me about their demons. Who kept their addictions going strong because they refused to get help. They couldn't get help. They needed help. I couldn't do anything about it.

"What the hell is this?" I asked, my voice hollow as I set the open bottle and the glass down on the counter. "You told me that the last time you had a drink was four years ago! You told me that you were sober! You fucking lied to me!"

Guilt flashed across his face, but it was quickly replaced by anger. He crossed his arms, and, at that moment, I saw the ugly beast that addiction brought out in people.

"Who said that I have to tell you everything? I slipped once, Addie! Once! You're going to stand there and act like I'm throwing away everything because I had one drink?"

I scoffed and shook my head. "You're an addict, Zane. And not one who's been in recovery long-term. You've been in a few years, and that's great, but you were feeling low, and you turned to drinking again."

"I can have one drink without it being a massive problem!"

"You drank half the damn bottle!" I said, gesturing at the bottle on the counter. "Half! When did you even do this? When I was sleeping last night? What did you do? Get off the phone with your sponsor and decide, hey, let's do the one thing I shouldn't be doing right now?"

"It's not like that, Addie," he said, pinching the bridge of his nose. When he looked back up at me, there was barely contained fury in his eyes.

"Then enlighten me!"

"Get out."

"You know what, I could have dealt with the addiction. I told you that I was going to go through this with you, but you lied to me again."

"I thought I told you to get out!" he yelled.

"Done," I said, trying to hold back the tears that blurred my vision. "I hope you get help, and I hope you can get right with yourself again, Zane. If you do or you want help, call me. I'll be there for you."

"I don't care. Just get out of my house and stop trying to fix me!"

I walked out of the house, not bothering to gather the things I had left there over the course of our relationship. I would get them later when both of us could be in the same room together without yelling at each other.

As I got in my car, I let the first tears fall. Once they started falling, they wouldn't stop. I hit the wheel as hard as I could, trying to drive some of the frustration out of my body.

When the tears stopped falling, I started the car and drove

away.

I couldn't let him drag me down with him.

Chapter 9

Zane

Two weeks was a long time to go without drinking. It was miserable.

I had been drinking for a week before Addie had found the evidence of my self-destruction. It had started off as one drink late at night, and then it had started spiraling out of control. Before I realized what was happening, the first bottle was gone. Then the fifth bottle was gone. Then the seventh.

It was only when she walked out and left me behind that I realized what I had done.

With one drink, I had managed to ruin my life again.

The day she walked out was the day I dumped the bourbon down the sink. I went to work and then home again, not stopping at the bar or anywhere that served alcohol—other than the grocery store where I bought a new bottle every day.

I don't know why, but I would head into town after finishing at the clinic just to buy a bottle of whatever I found first before heading home. I would then line up the unopened bottle on the counter with the several others I had bought and convince myself that I didn't need to drink them.

It was my favorite form of torture, apparently.

When I got home from work, I added the fourteenth bottle to the line. I didn't even like tequila, but somehow, I purchased three bottles of it.

"Fuck," I muttered as I looked at the bottles. I wanted to crack their seals and start drinking, but I couldn't.

Every day I thought about calling Fleur or going over to her home a few feet away from me and admit I was struggling. I thought about telling her that I had fallen for her daughter before I ruined everything. And then I thought about the look that would be on her face when I told her that.

I grabbed one of the bottles and grabbed the top, ready to twist the seal. When I looked across the kitchen at where Addie had last stood, all I could see was her disappointed face. I could see the hurt on her face when I told her to get out of my house.

When I put the bottle back down, I could hear the addiction calling my name again. I took a deep breath before taking several steps away from the counter. I had thrown away four years of sobriety. Instead of going to the meetings and talking to Fleur, I drowned my sorrows in alcohol and hoped that nobody would notice.

I had known from the beginning that I would ruin everything between Addie and me. As it turned out, I was a self-fulfilling prophecy.

"What the hell are you doing wallowing in your own pity?" Fleur said as she stormed into my house, looking like the hounds of hell were on her heels. "Is this really going to help anything?"

"Go away, Fleur. I didn't give you the key so you could barge your way in here and tell me what to do."

"And I didn't sponsor your ass through sobriety and watch my daughter fall for you to let you throw everything away like this. Now get your ass over to the couch. We're going to talk about this whether you like it or not."

"Get out!" I shouted, feeling the panic rising in my chest.

Fleur snorted and sat down on the couch. "Don't try the angry addict shit with me, young man. I've been there and done that. Now, get your ass on the couch and start talking!"

I scowled at her but stalked over to the couch across from her and sat down. When I kicked my feet up on the coffee table, Fleur sent me a withering look. I dropped my feet from the table and sat up straighter.

"You're acting like a petulant child," Fleur said as she crossed one leg over the other.

"I feel like a petulant child," I said with a sigh, running a hand through my hair. "I don't know what to do, Fleur. I've screwed up everything. I started drinking because I couldn't deal with the anniversary date, and then it just started spiraling from there."

"The anniversary date is the only reason you started drinking again?" Fleur asked, her soft accent soothing as she spoke. "Zane, I've watched you make it through other years without even considering picking up a bottle."

"I don't know. There's been a lot going on in my life the last few months."

"You hid your addiction from someone you cared about," Fleur said. "That takes a toll on you. It puts more stress on you, and you end up in an endless loop of what happens when they find out, and you can't tell them because they will be so hurt and disappointed and maybe angry."

"I really ruined things with her," I said, swallowing the lump in my throat.

"You did. But there's a quality about my daughter that I find amazing. She forgives people. Too often, sometimes. But no matter how bad you think you've ruined things with her, I can pretty much promise you that you haven't."

"I don't even know how to apologize to her."

"Don't worry about apologizing to her yet. We do not get sober for other people. It doesn't last. You have to want to get sober again for yourself. Do you want to?"

"It isn't that easy," I said, running my hands down my face. I didn't know what I was supposed to do. Drinking numbed the pain. I wanted the pain to keep being numb.

"You do know what to do," Fleur said. "You know that it's a

choice you have to make for yourself and nobody else. No matter what you choose, you know you're going to have my support."

"I appreciate that."

"I'm going to be honest with you," Fleur said, shifting on the couch and crossing her legs beneath her. "I want to see you want to get sober again, Zane. It wasn't easy the first time, and it isn't going to be easy this time."

"I haven't had a drink in two weeks."

"Good." Fleur nodded and pulled her phone out of her pocket, looking at something. She looked up at me with a small smile. "There's a meeting tonight."

"I don't know if I'm ready for that."

Fleur tucked her phone back in her pocket. "You don't have to go, but I think it would be a good idea even if you don't talk. Hearing how other people are struggling will make you feel like you're less alone in this battle."

I looked down at my hands, clenching and unclenching my fists. Part of me wanted to go to the meeting, and part of me didn't. I didn't want to hear how other people had it worse than I did, and I didn't want to talk about my own life. All I wanted to do was crawl back into my hole and start drinking again.

"Can we go now?" I asked, knowing that if she gave me more time to think about it, I wouldn't go.

"Go get ready, and we'll go for dinner before we go to the meeting."

Not for the first time, I was grateful that Fleur was in my life. She wasn't going to let me slip through the cracks, even if I wanted to head dive into them.

***

The morning after a meeting was easier for me than other mornings. I felt better after talking to the others and listening to them talk about going through the same struggles I was going through.

However, by the time it came time to head home from work, I was feeling horrible. Two patients needed an oncologist referral. Giving the news to someone that they needed to see a specialist and that I couldn't help them always hit me hard.

"Time to call it a day?" Van asked as he looked up from his filing. "You look like you've been having a horrible time."

"I'm fine," I said, gritting my teeth and putting the last of my files from the day on his desk.

"Are you?" Van asked, quirking one eyebrow. "Because based on the bottle of vodka I saw in your garbage the other day, you're not doing okay at all. Do you want to lose your practice?"

"It was a bottle from a few weeks ago. I haven't had a drink in fifteen days, and it's driving me insane, but I'm doing it."

"Good," Van said, his face brightening into a smile. "I'm glad you're taking care of yourself. You let me know if you need anything."

"Will do," I said, knowing that I wouldn't call him if I needed anything.

Van smiled and nodded, turning back to his work as I made my way to the door.

What I wanted to do after my shift was head to the bar and have a drink. Or go see Addie and beg for her forgiveness. Ask for her help. Fleur was right, though. I have to do this for me. I can't get sober again and have it all fall apart the moment she and I had another problem in our relationship.

If I'm doing this, it has to be for me. It has to be to save my own life.

On the way home, I stopped at the grocery store, craving something to drink. I walked up and down the two aisles filled with alcohol, looking for something that would suit my mood.

This is only a stage of life you're going through. Get your shit together and get out of here.

I sighed and ran my hand through my hair. I picked up a bottle and read the label, pretending that I cared about where the alcohol came from before putting it back on the shelf.

I can do this. Walk away.

After taking a deep breath, I turned and walked back to my truck. I got in and stared at the grocery store for a long time, considering going back in. I wanted to go back in. Everything in me was screaming at me to go back inside, pick a bottle of anything, and head home.

Instead, I started the engine and headed home. I wasn't going to give in to the cravings today. I had to be stronger than the cravings.

I'm doing this for me.

When I got home, I took the first bottle out of the lineup and poured it down the drain. Once I looked at the other bottles, I sank to the floor with my head in my hands. I wanted to pour out the rest of the bottles, but I couldn't get myself up off the floor to do it.

I need those bottles. I can't get rid of them yet. I need them. What if I need a drink?

I hated myself at that moment. I hated myself for needing to keep the alcohol and not being strong enough to dump them all.

After taking a deep breath, I pulled out my phone and sent Fleur a message.

She burst through my door a few moments later, sinking to the ground and pulling me into her arms. "It's okay. You're okay. You're not weak. You're so strong, Zane. You were able to pour out one of the bottles. That's more than you could have done yesterday. I'm so proud of you."

"I've never felt weaker," I said, a lump catching in my throat. I swallowed hard and took a deep breath. "Why couldn't I pour out all the bottles? Why do I feel like I still need them?"

"Because they gave you comfort when nothing else could, but you have so much more to live for now. You don't need those bottles sitting around and cluttering up your life, but you don't have to get rid of them until you're ready."

"That's okay?"

"Honey," Fleur said, holding me closer as tears dripped down my cheeks. "Whatever you need to do to heal is okay."

I nodded and took a deep breath. "Will you help me pour the rest of the bottles out? I don't think I can do it by myself."

"Absolutely," she said, getting up and helping me to my feet.

Together we poured out the bottles, watching as the liquid disappeared down the drain. I felt one step closer to my sobriety with every bottle we poured out. I was one step closer to getting better, and that's all it took.

Baby steps.

I could do this.

Chapter 10

Addie

Three weeks passed without a single word from Zane. I hadn't expected to hear anything from him, although I had hoped. I thought that he might reach out and say something once he started feeling better, but he didn't. There was no word from him. To be fair, I didn't reach out to him either.

I was busy sorting through classroom decorations when my mother walked into my apartment like it was her own home. I grinned at her and got up, wrapping her in a hug.

"You finally have time to decorate your classroom?" Mom asked as she took a seat on the floor and started picking through some of the decorations.

"In another week or two, I'm going in on one of the weekends. I just have to figure out what theme I want to have."

"Have you thought any more about going to see him?" Mom asked, picking up a drawing one of my students had done for me years ago.

"I've thought about it over and over again, Mom. I don't want to butt into his life, and I don't want to be around him if he's still drinking."

"You know, I've been in recovery for the last ten years, and it still doesn't get any easier."

The world fell out from beneath me as I looked at my mother. "I didn't know."

"It was easy to hide from you. Your last couple years of high school weren't spent at home much, and once you got into university, you barely came home. There was plenty of time to fight the alcohol addiction and get into recovery without ever having to have that conversation with me."

I ran my hand through my hair and stared up at my mother. It was a lot to take in all at once. I hadn't known that she was struggling with alcohol when I was in high school. I had been completely oblivious to it. There was no way that I should have missed that, but I did.

"I'm sorry I didn't know," I said, blinking back the tears that blurred my vision.

"I didn't want you to know," Mom said. "I hid it from you, but I got sober. I've been in recovery for the last ten years. I've turned my life around, but it wasn't easy. I almost screwed it up a few times. Don't be so hard on him. He's struggling in a way that I hope you will never fully understand."

"He lied to me, Mom."

"Addicts lie," she said, reaching out to brush a strand of hair back from my face. "He's been sober for twenty-one days. He's going to meetings every day. He's working hard to get himself okay again."

"Why are you telling me that?" I shook my head. "He doesn't want me around. He told me to get out."

"Addie, the way you look at him tells me all I need to know about how you feel about him. And he told you to get out because he's ashamed."

I crossed my legs and stared down at the mess of decorations in front of me. It seemed easier to look at them than to try and look at my mother while I processed everything.

The way I felt for Zane *was* unlike anything I had ever felt for anybody else, but I didn't know that it had been that obvious.

"How's he doing other than trying to stay sober?" I asked, looking up at her.

"He's not doing great. He misses you just as much as you miss him. He knows that you have to do what's best for you, though."

I nodded and changed the subject, talking about possible classroom things with her instead of talking about Zane. Talking about him hurt too much. I didn't give him a chance before walking out on him. I knew what addicts were like, and I still walked away when he was screaming for help.

Guilt twisted and turned my stomach. I kept a hold of my emotions until my mom left, and I was finally alone. As soon as she was gone, I raced to my room and got changed.

I should have been helping Zane when he needed me the most. Instead, I had let him push me away, thinking his addiction would turn him into a monster like my ex-husband. I had closed my eyes to everything I knew about Zane and pretended that he was a different person entirely.

I left him on his own to fight.

As soon as I was dressed, I grabbed my keys and drove to his place. The entire drive, I drummed my fingers on the wheel, trying to think of what I was going to say to him when I got there. An apology seemed like a good place to start, but I didn't know what would come after that.

Would I ask him to forgive me for leaving him when he needed me?

Would I send him spiraling into a drinking binge that would ruin his sobriety?

Would we decide that there was no saving what we had already lost?

There was no way to know what would happen unless I got out of the car, marched myself up to his door, and demanded that he talk to me no matter what the outcome might be. He and I both needed some sort of future or closure. No matter how our conversation went, we couldn't just leave things hanging in the air and wait for whatever came next.

After I took a deep breath and tried to convince myself that this wouldn't be the worst conversation of the year, I walked to the door and rang the bell. I could hear movement on the other side of the door, and I was sure that Zane was looking at me through the peephole. I shifted my weight from one side to the other.

When the door opened, my breath caught in my throat. Zane's cheeks were hollow, and there were dark bags beneath his eyes. I looked him over, looking at the way his clothes hung loosely off his body.

"How are you doing?" I asked, looking over him again. He was paler than he was before, and he looked exhausted.

"Better than I was."

I nodded, my mouth going dry as my heart raced. "I'm sorry."

"I don't think you have any reason to be sorry," he said, giving me a small smile. "I'm the one who kicked you out and lied to you."

"And I'm the one who didn't ask you what was wrong or offer to help you. I think we've both got things to apologize for right now."

"I'm sorry, Addie."

"Well, now that we've both said we're sorry, I want to know how to help you. Can you explain everything to me?" I rubbed the back of my neck and shifted my weight again, feeling my cheeks warm up. "If you're comfortable talking about it."

"Come in," he said, opening the door wider.

When he opened the door, I saw a box of my belongings sitting on the entryway table. A sharp pain radiated through my chest as I looked at everything I had left with him condensed into a small box. It seemed so final, like nothing that I could say or do at this point would help us recover.

"I didn't know when you would come to get those things," Zane said, his voice a little more than a whisper as he looked down at me. "You didn't come and get them for so long that I thought there was still some hope, but now you're here."

"I'm not here to leave you again," I said, looking up at him. "I'm here to be with you in whatever way you need right now."

He nodded, his jaw tense as he led the way to the couches. He sat down on one, leaving the other for me. I sat down and tried to calm my racing heart as I waited for him to say something first. The indecision was clear on his face. His mouth opened and closed several times without anything coming out.

"Whatever you need to say to me about what happened or what will happen, just say it. I want everything out in the open, so we can start working through it."

"I need a partner, Addie. Someone who isn't going to run when I start struggling with my alcohol addiction."

"And I need a partner who isn't going to lie to me or hide things from me when they're struggling. I want to be there for you, Zane, but I can't be there if you don't let me know what's happening."

"We've both made a mess of things between us, haven't we?"

"Yes, we have," I said, pulling my legs up to sit cross-legged on the couch. "That's why I'm asking you what you need me to do to help you get through this."

Zane didn't meet my eyes once as he looked around the room. He twisted his hands in his lap. I held my breath, waiting for him to speak. I needed him to tell me that there was a way we could work through this.

"This is new ground for both of us," he said before wincing. "Well, maybe not you."

"It is new," I said. "Your addiction and your problems are not the same as somebody else's."

Zane took a deep breath and nodded. "Well then, you should probably know more about why I broke my sobriety."

"Whatever you're willing to tell me."

He got up and sat on the couch beside me, twisting slightly in his seat to face me. I shifted my own position, leaning back against the arm of the couch and looking at him.

"The anniversary is always hard for me, but most years, I can handle it. I do everything I can to stay busy, so I don't have time to think about the bottle. This year, I got an email from the girl's father. I'm not going to go into all the details about it, but he was basically blaming me for the loss of his daughter and telling me about the other ways I destroyed his family."

"It was an accident, though. Surgeries go wrong, and patients die," I said, reaching out to put my hand on his knee. "You couldn't have controlled the situation."

"There's a lot I could have done differently."

"There's a lot anybody could have done differently in any given situation. It doesn't mean that it's going to change the outcome."

His lips twitched. "You sound like my sponsor."

"Well, my mom is a smart woman."

"She told you."

I nodded. "She told me."

Zane sighed and put his hand over mine, squeezing it lightly. "After getting that email, I started to spiral even more out of control. At night I was restless. I couldn't sleep, and even if I managed to fall asleep for a few hours, all I could see was Lily's face after the life drained out of her. All I could hear were her parents' screams as I told them that their daughter had died."

"How are you feeling right now?" I asked, flipping my hand over and lacing my fingers through his. "Are you alright talking about this?"

"I want to go get a drink, but it's nothing that I can't handle right now."

"What do you need from me?"

He looked hesitant as he squeezed my hand again. "Will you come with me to a meeting tonight?"

"Of course," I said as I kneeled in front of him and pulled him into a tight hug.

Zane held onto me, his arms tight around my waist as I heard his first sob. He buried his face in my neck and fell apart. I stayed in his embrace, willing to hold him together until he could hold himself together.

"I'm here for you. We're going to get through this, and I'm going to support you through it all."

Chapter 11

Zane

I flipped the sixty-day sobriety chip over in my hand. It wasn't the first time that I had earned the chip, but it didn't make it any less important. I had made it sixty days without taking a single drink. I had done the impossible, and I was coming out on the other side.

Even as I looked at the chip, I knew that I could only take it one day at a time. I wanted to get better, but thinking about anything more than tomorrow made my stomach toss and turn.

All I had to do was make it one more day sober and then another day after that.

It was going to take time, as Fleur liked to constantly remind me when we talked. She offered her time and supported me the same way she had when she helped me get sober the first time.

Addie had gone with me to every single meeting since we reconnected. Even on the nights I didn't want her to come in with me, she sat in the truck or her car and waited for me to come back out. She showed up at my house early in the mornings. She had stayed over to go running. When she said she was going to be there for me, she meant it.

"Congratulations," Addie said as she met me outside. Snow started falling down around us as she hugged me tightly.

I dipped my head down to kiss her before we walked back to the truck. She had been asking me about the blankets and pillows in the back of the truck for the better part of the day, but I hadn't told her. It had taken me a few days to plan the surprise for her, and I wasn't going to let her ruin that surprise by asking a million questions.

"Let's go to dinner to celebrate," Addie said as we got in the truck. "My treat."

"We don't have to do that," I said as I started the engine.

I smiled despite what I said. I was happy that she wanted to celebrate the little things, but it didn't feel like that big of an accomplishment. I was only sixty days sober after having four years of sobriety under my belt.

It was bittersweet.

"I want to if you want to. We should celebrate your successes."

She was right, even if I had mixed feelings about it.

"It's only sixty days sober."

"And it's an accomplishment that you fought for. Now, stop arguing with me and take me to wherever you want to eat for dinner."

I laughed as I shook my head, warmth spreading through my body as I drove down to my favorite diner. Addie sang along with the radio, drumming her fingers on the armrest and bobbing her head. As I glanced at her, I knew that I was head over heels for her.

When we got to the diner, Addie stood in the parking lot for a few minutes, tilting her head back and looking up at the falling snow. I stood behind her, wrapping my arms around her and kissing her cheek.

"Come on, I'm starving, and I have a surprise for you that we can't miss."

"Oh, really?" Addie asked, smiling at me as she wriggled her way out of my embrace and took my hand. "Let's go eat then."

"Well," I said, pulling her back to me. She wrapped her arms around my neck, pressing herself closer to me. "There's something you should know first."

"And what might that be?"

"I love you," I said, brushing a strand of hair behind her ear. "I know we've only known each other for a few months, but I love you so damn much."

"I love you too," Addie said, standing up on her toes and pressing her lips against mine.

I kissed her back, pulling her as close to my body as she could get. When we pulled apart, she looked like she was floating on air as we walked into the diner. As I watched her enter the diner, I could imagine walking into the diner with her every week for the rest of our lives.

***

"Are you finally going to tell me what we're doing out here?" Addie asked as I parked at a lookoff.

It was dark out, but the snow had stopped falling. We were in the mountains at one of my favorite places in the world. The lookoff was a safe place for me. Somewhere I came whenever I needed some time alone to think about major decisions in my life.

"You can see so much of the valley from here," Addie said, walking toward the edge of the lookoff. She leaned against the railing and looked down. "Come over here with me. You have to see this view."

"In a minute," I said, reaching into the back of the truck and digging out the blankets and pillows. I tossed them onto the bed of the truck, spreading them out before joining her at the railing.

"So, why are we up here?"

"There's a meteor shower that should be happening soon. We will cuddle in the back of my truck to make some wishes on shooting stars."

"They're not really shooting stars, though."

"Shush, woman," I said, picking her up and tossing her over my shoulder. I smacked her ass as I carried her to the truck. Addie laughed as I lowered her onto the tailgate and stood between her legs.

"I love you," she whispered.

I grinned and kissed her. Our mouths slanted together as her legs circled my waist. I moaned as she pressed herself against the erection straining against my jeans. She rolled her hips, pressing harder against me.

"The meteor shower is about to start," she said, pulling away from me to point at the sky. I looked up and saw the first few meteors begin to fall.

"Good," I said as she drew away from me and crawled further into the bed of the truck, leaning into the pillows. I crawled after her, hovering over her body.

Heat burned bright in her eyes as she reached for the zipper on my jacket. Snow started falling around us as we shed our clothes. When she was naked, I kissed my way down her body until I got to her breasts. I took one nipple in my mouth, tweaking the other as her nails raked down my back. I groaned as her fingers threaded through my hair, pulling my face up to hers.

I reached between us, toying with her clit as I kissed her, our tongues tangling. She nipped at my lips, smoothing her tongue over the stinging sensation before working her way down to my neck.

As she kissed my neck, she gripped my cock. I nearly came in her hand as she stroked me, smoothing her thumb over the head. She stroked me in time with me thrusting my fingers in her wetness, wriggling as her orgasm started to build. When I looked down at her, seeing the expression on her face, it only made me harder.

"Fuck, baby," I moaned, pulling back from her slightly. I grabbed her hands and pinned them above her head, the head of my cock against her entrance.

As I slid inside her, she arched her back. I grabbed a pillow and lifted her hips, stuffing it beneath them before thrusting. When I let go of her hands, she held onto me, her nails raking down my back again.

I kissed my way back down to her breasts as I was thrusting. She writhed against me as I nipped at her nipples before taking one into my mouth. As I sucked and nipped her, she bucked against me.

When I slipped one hand between us to play with her clit, she came apart again, my name on her lips. I groaned, grabbing her hip, and thrusting harder until I came.

"I missed that," she said as I lay beside her.

"Me too," I said.

I pulled the blankets over us before pulling her against my body. Addie sighed as she nestled against me, looking up at the night sky.

Meteors were falling all around us, bright streaks against the sky. I kissed Addie's temple, holding her against me tighter.

"I can't believe you brought me up here to watch meteors," Addie said, kissing my shoulder. "I love it. Nobody has ever done anything like this for me before."

"We can come up here and stare at the stars as much as you like."

"Promise," she asked, looking up at me.

"I promise."

Addie snuggled against me again, her hand moving softly up and down the planes of my stomach. I wrapped my arms tighter around her, holding her closer. She was everything that I had ever wanted and more. Everything would be alright if I kept her safe in my arms. We would be alright, even after all that we had gone through at the beginning of our relationship.

"Make a wish," Addie whispered, her voice soft.

I could make a million different wishes, but all of them had something to do with her. Everything that had to do with our future together flashed through my mind. They were all wishes that I hoped would come true, but I couldn't settle on any of those ideas.

Instead, I settled on what was true at that moment.

"I wish that this night would never end."

Addie smiled and propped herself up on one arm to look down at me. "We're going to have thousands of nights even better than this one."

Chapter 12

Addie

It had taken several weeks, but I finally had a time when I could drag in all my classroom decorations. Of course, it was while the students were all on Christmas break, but that didn't matter to me. I would have a new classroom by the time they came back after the new year. We would be able to start entirely fresh. It would be new and exciting for the kindergarteners, and I couldn't wait.

Tearing down the old decorations had taken most of the morning, even with Zane helping me. He gathered the pieces of paper and broken supplies, tossing them into the garbage as I sorted through the things I didn't want that could be given to other teachers.

"So," Zane said as he carried the last garbage bag to the door. "What is the theme going to be?"

"I'm thinking jungle safari," I said, abandoning my donation pile to rifle through the decorations I had brought with me. "Look at how cute this is."

Zane looked at the cut-out of a tiger and chuckled. "That thing is massive. Where are you even going to put it?"

I grinned and took the tiger over to the wall beneath the whiteboard. It stood as tall as an actual tiger, and I had spent more money on it than I was willing to admit. The money didn't matter, though. I loved seeing the smiles on the kids' faces. I could already see the smiles on their faces as we picked a name for the tiger together.

"Right here," I said, holding it up against the wall. "They're going to go insane when they see it."

Zane grabbed the stapler I had tossed on one of the tables. He handed it to me and took my place, holding the front half of the tiger against the wall. I started stapling it in place, laughing as Zane pretended that he was trying to hold a wild tiger back.

"You're crazy," I said after I put the last staple into the tiger.

Zane wrapped his arms around me and pulled me to him. "Crazy about you."

I stood on my toes and kissed him, shaking my head when his hands slipped into my back pockets. "You know, once the new year comes, I'm about to get busier teaching. I'll have to work on lesson plans more at night."

"You can work on lesson plans all you want," he said. "I might even learn how to cook something other than boxed mac and cheese, so you don't have to worry about feeding us every night."

Laughing, I pulled away from him. "You don't have to do that. I like cooking."

"I want to do that, Addie. We're partners, remember? You're going to support me, and I'm going to support you. Either way, at my age, I should know how to cook something other than meat on a grill and mac and cheese."

"Alright," I said, going back to my donation pile. "I'll teach you how to cook if you agree to help me move once I find a new place."

"When are you moving?" he asked.

"My lease ends next month. It was only a short one since I didn't know whether I was going to buy a house or not."

"Well, if you're looking for somewhere to live, I know a place. It's beautiful. Backs right onto the woods. It's about a forty-minute drive away from town, though."

"It sounds nice," I said. "But I don't know if I could afford the mortgage on a house right now on my own."

"Who said you would be on your own?" Zane asked as he wrapped his arm around me. "Do you want to go see the place?"

"Can we go after we're done setting everything up? I really want to get the room done today so we can enjoy the rest of Christmas break together."

"Of course," he said, digging into the donation pile and helping me sort through it. "Let's get everything done, and then we can go."

He and I worked through the pile of decorations, stapling them to the walls until my classroom looked like it had been turned into a jungle safari. Toucans and monkeys were placed up high, spreading their wings and flying through the tree cut-outs.

"It looks amazing," I said, grinning as I pulled Zane into a tight hug. "Thank you so much for helping me."

"Addie, I'd do anything for you. You know that, right?"

I smiled up at him and ran my fingers along his jaw. "I'm starting to see that."

"Why don't we go take a look at that house I was telling you about?"

I nodded and took his hand, pulling him to the door. Even if I couldn't afford the house, it wouldn't hurt to start getting ideas about what I wanted when I searched for another place.

Besides, his excitement was contagious.

***

My mouth dropped when Zane turned off the highway and into a driveway. The entire front of the property was lined with trees, as was the winding driveway that worked its way toward the house.

As the house came into view, I started falling in love. The front of the house was almost entirely made of glass and white stone. It was stunning. The house looked like it had been designed specifically for this property.

"Want to go inside?" Zane asked as he stopped the truck and pulled a key out of his pocket.

"How did you get a key to this place?"

"Well, I might have bought it and finished building it a few months ago. I wasn't quite ready to move into it yet, but if your lease is ending and you want to, you could come live here with me."

"You want me to move in with you?" I asked, not quite believing what he was saying.

"Of course," he said, getting out of the truck. He rounded the front of the truck and opened my door, helping me out. "I would love if you came to live with me."

I grinned and kissed him. "I would love to live with you."

"Then let me show you the rest of our new house."

Zane took me by the hand and led me to the backyard. There was a pool, a hot tub, a massive patio, and a deck, both filled with patio furniture and meant for entertaining. The property backed onto the woods, a trail starting at the treeline.

When we went inside, I nearly squealed. The floors were pale, and the walls were dark and moody. The walls were almost entirely glass. The kitchen was huge, and it overlooked the backyard.

Zane led me to the master bedroom, and I fell in love with the bathroom attached to it. The large tub sat beside a wall made of windows that overlooked the forest.

"Do you want to see the other bedrooms?" he asked as he laced his fingers through mine.

"There's more?"

He nodded. "Of course, there is. I want to have children someday. I want a big family with kids and dogs and any other animal you want."

Tears blurred my vision as I smiled at him. "Kids, dogs, cats, and maybe a couple of chickens."

Zane laughed and pulled me into a tight hug. "I'll call around tomorrow and find out if Van knows anyone that makes a good chicken coop. Knowing him, he probably does."

"We're really going to do this?" I asked, looking at him and wondering how long he had been thinking about this.

"We're really going to do this," Zane said. He stepped out of the hug and took my hand again. "I have something else to show you out back on that little trail."

We walked across the property to the trailhead. Zane led the way down the trailhead, talking about the furniture shopping we were going to need to do. Between the two of us, we could fill some of the rooms but not all of them. I grinned, already picturing how I was going to decorate the nursery.

Zane stopped along the path and led me several feet off the trail and into a small clearing. Flower petals were scattered across the snow, and there was a pair of benches with a fire pit in the middle.

"This is ours too?" I asked, looking around at the little clearing. I could already see lights draped through the surrounding trees and nights spent out here falling more in love with each other than we already were.

"Yeah, it is." He kissed my cheek. "Now close your eyes and wait until I tell you to open them again."

"There's more?" I asked, my eyes wide.

"Close your eyes, Addie."

I laughed and did as he said, waiting as the cold air seeped through my jacket. I shifted my weight from side to side, trying to keep warm as I heard rustling behind me.

"Open your eyes," he said. "And then turn around."

I opened my eyes and turned around, my hands flying to cover my mouth as I looked down at him. Zane was on one knee with a little velvet box open in his hand. There was a ring nestled inside the box, gleaming in the last rays of sunlight.

"Addie Manning, I fell in love with you a thousand times since the day I found you in that hole. I knew months ago that I would never love another woman the way I loved you. Hell, I couldn't picture my life without you. I know this is soon, but when you know, you know. I've never been any more certain of anything in my life."

"Yes!" I squealed, nearly knocking him into the snow as I hugged and kissed him tightly.

Zane was laughing when I pulled away. "You didn't even let me ask the question."

"Doesn't matter," I said before kissing him again. "I knew I wanted to spend the rest of my life with you months ago."

"Still," he said, brushing a strand of hair behind my ear. "I want to do this properly."

"Then ask," I said, cupping his face in my hands. "I've never loved someone the way I love you."

"Addie, will you marry me?"

"Yes!"

Zane's grin could have lit up the darkest corners of the world as he smiled and slipped the ring on my finger. I looked down at it, smiling before I kissed him again.

"Can we get out of the cold now and go home?" I asked as we stood up.

"Or," he said, his hot breath grazing across my ear as he hugged me from behind. "We could go start christening the new house. I was thinking we could start with the kitchen."

I grinned and leaned back into him. "Race you there?"

"You're on."

We took off running through the snow, laughing and shouting like we were children again. I had never been happier in my life.

When we got back to the house, he swept me into his arms and carried me to the kitchen, ready to start the rest of our lives together.

Epilogue

Zane

Two and a half years later

Smoke from the barbecue scented the warm summer air. Music was playing softly in the background as our family and friends celebrated the end of summer and the start of a new little life in the town.

"That smells delicious," Addie said as she walked over to me, nestling into my side. Her hand drifted down to her stomach. I grinned as I kissed her temple. "I could eat a dozen of them."

"Should I make another dozen of them for the baby too?"

Addie laughed and elbowed my side. "Funny. As much as I could eat twelve burgers, I don't think I'm going to. My stomach is in knots."

"It's only a gender reveal," I said, running my fingers through her hair. "We're going to find out whether we're having a little boy or girl."

"Your mom is going to lose her mind if we have a boy," Addie said, glancing over at my mother, who was wandering around my backyard and telling everyone who would listen that we had to be having a son.

"I'll be happy as long as we have a healthy baby."

She nodded and leaned closer to my side, her head leaning into my chest. I ran my fingers along her hip, the feeling of her dress silky and smooth. As I stood there with her, I knew that life had worked out exactly how it was meant to be.

"How do you feel with the anniversary coming up in a few months?" Addie asked.

"I'm doing okay. It's getting easier. We'll see three years sober."

Addie smiled and reached up to run her fingers along my jaw. I leaned into her touch as I smiled down at her.

"I'm so proud of you and all you've accomplished," Addie said. "I don't know how we wouldn't have gotten this far otherwise."

"I'm just happy that you came back and stuck around."

"I'm happy that you let me in and let me love you. And that we only have four more months until we get to meet our little baby."

"Speaking of the baby," Fleur said as she appeared out of nowhere. "Why don't we go cut the cake and see what the baby's going to be now?"

"Can't hold back, can you?" Addie asked, her tone teasing as she left me to loop her arm through her mother's. "Lead the way to the cake!"

I followed my wife of nearly a year and a half to the cake, grinning at how she waddled with her pregnant belly. Together we stood beside the cake. People were laughing and talking as they all made predictions about the baby.

"Are you ready?" I asked, wrapping my arm around Addie's waist as she picked up the knife.

"Not even a little bit," Addie said, a line appearing between her eyebrows. "What if I'm not a good mother?"

"You're going to be an amazing mother. Now, cut the cake and tell me that I was right about having a girl."

Addie rolled her eyes, but her smile grew. She cut a thick slice out of the white cake and pulled it out, revealing a pink interior.

"I was right," I whispered as tears started rolling down her cheeks.

"It's a girl!" she yelled, grinning from ear to ear.

Our families and friends cheered as Addie put down the piece of cake and the knife. She turned to kiss me, tears still streaming down her face. My vision was blurry as we pulled apart to a sea of people rushing to congratulate us.

I had never felt surrounded by more love.

If anybody had told me three years ago that I would meet and marry the woman of my dreams, I wouldn't have believed them. I thought I was destined to be alone for everything I had done. My life had only been getting worse before she walked in and changed everything for me.

Now, as I held her in my arms with our baby on the way, I knew that life could only get better.

- END -

If you enjoyed *Mountain Man Doctor*, take a look at a sneak peek of the final book in the series: *Mountain Man Handyman.*

Prologue
Della

"I can't do this anymore," I whispered, my eyes wet. I looked at Greer, his expression marred by a frown. He was just as upset. I could see it in the redness rimming his eyes. He was angry, too, and I couldn't really blame him.

"Do what?" he asked, throwing his arms up in defeat. "Be with me?"

It'd been a year since his parents died, and while I helped him through it as best I could, I could no longer pretend I was happy. But he wouldn't understand. He already thought my decision had something to do with him when it didn't. Not really.

I licked my lips. They were wet and salty from my tears. I was trying my hardest to stem them, not when it felt like my heart was shattering inside my chest. I attempted to inhale a full breath, but I couldn't manage that either. Greer pulled his hand through his hair, visibly confused and frustrated, and I couldn't, in any way, blame him for how he was feeling.

"I need more, Greer. This..." I waved my hand around my grandmother's cabin, "...isn't enough anymore." Nanna's cabin was a metaphor, though, for Kipsty Little Town itself, the small town we called home.

Greer expelled an angry sigh, looking between me and my luggage. I was planning on leaving before he came home, which I realized may have been cowardly, but I wanted to spare us this pain. I didn't have the courage to face Greer before I left, and had written him a note instead, but he surprised me by coming home early for the weekend. He was studying Landscape Architecture at Colorado University and could only manage to come home on a Friday afternoon and stay for the weekend. It was another reason I couldn't keep doing this and why I needed to leave. He was at school all week, and it felt as though all I really did was wait for him to come so we could spend a morsel of time together.

"Is it me?" he asked. His voice cracked, making me feel worse than I already did. I wasn't only breaking my 18-year-old heart. I was breaking his too. And as much as it killed me, I couldn't keep lying to myself anymore. Kipsty Little Town had become too small. I'd lived here my whole life, and all I'd ever really wanted was to leave and find something bigger. And, to some degree, something better, I guess. I felt trapped here, stuck on a hamster wheel that kept spinning without going anywhere. If I tried to explain to Greer the restlessness that had resided under my skin, and in my veins, for the last year, he wouldn't understand.

I took a step toward him, and he matched it by taking a step away from me. The physical distance between us hurt, I loved him with every part of me, but our emotional distance was fraught with tightly bound tension on the verge of snapping us in two. And that, I realized, was what hurt the most. I had loved this boy from the time I was fifteen, he'd been my first everything, and it brought me no pleasure at all to inflict any kind of hurt on him. But three years later, I had to do what was best for me, and this town, staying here, was not it. But Greer wasn't listening to me. This had almost nothing to do with him, yet in his eyes, I was leaving because of him. That couldn't be further from the cold, hard truth.

"It's not about you," I replied, swiping at the tears sliding down my cheeks. I had to find a way to pull myself together and stay strong in my own conviction. "I love you," I told him fervently. "I'm in love with you. But I can't stay here, Greer. I'm unhappy, and I'm not like you. I can't see my future in this godforsaken podunk town. I want more for my life than being stuck here and living the same life my grandmother has lived."

My life in Kipsty wasn't bad. It had never been. I was raised by a very strong woman who profoundly influenced the woman I'd become. And as much as it hurt my grandmother to see me leave, she understood, better than anyone, why I was doing it. My mother did the same thing when she was my age, except she showed up back here a year later with me in tow and dropped me off on my grandmother's porch. She never stuck around after that. And as much as I hated to admit it, the same restiveness that filled her spirit, existed in me, and it was about the only thing she gave me, besides my blonde hair, blue eyes, and curvy build.

Greer winced, and I watched him withdraw from me. It was like experiencing the loss of air in your lungs. And I was cold without him. Chilled to my marrow. He unknowingly took my air and heat and stepped away. The withdrawal was acute, and I felt it in every cell in my body. But I wouldn't cave. I wouldn't change my mind, and I think he was starting to realize that.

"Then I guess there's not much left for me to say," he told me quietly. For the briefest moment, he closed the gaping space between us, held my head between his strong and steady hands, kissed my forehead, and inhaled my scent one last time. I reveled in that affection, knowing it would most likely be the last.

"I hope you find what you're looking for, Del. I really do."

He stepped back and gave me one last look, his green eyes red and filled with so much I couldn't quite put a name to. He shook his head and walked towards the front door of the cabin I'd lived in my whole life. It was filled to the brim with memories. Memories I'd also have to leave behind once I was gone. It wouldn't serve me to hold on to anything if I wanted to move forward. The memories I'd keep were those of Nanna and me because they'd get me through the hard times ahead.

Greer glanced at me from over his shoulder and opened his mouth as if he had something else to say, but instead, he walked out and shut the door. I collapsed against the back of the sofa, and a sob escaped from between my lips. I slapped my hand over my mouth to smother the sound, but it was difficult when it felt like my lungs weren't working.

The pain in my chest intensified, and I looked up just in time to see my grandmother, Delia, stop between the living room and the kitchen. Without uttering a word, she opened her arms, and I rushed to her, seeking the kind of comfort only she could give me.

"I think I broke my own heart, Nanna," I cried, my head on her shoulder. She wrapped her arms around me, rubbing her hand over my back. "He'll never forgive me."

"Hush now," she replied. "You knew this was the hard part, Della." She pushed me back, hands on my shoulders. "You know in your heart of hearts that you won't be happy if you stay, and you'll only end up resenting that boy if you stay for him. You understand, baby girl?"

I nodded and swallowed the knot of tangled emotions clogging my throat. "Leaving you is hard, too," I told her. And it was. She raised me, gave me a beautiful life, and made sure I turned out to be a decent human being. Everyone in town loved her, but I was so damn lucky she was my family. I was who I was because she made me.

"I know," she replied gently. "But I want you to be happy, Della. You've been a dreamer your whole life, and I'd never stand in the way of those big dreams just to keep you here with me." Her eyes glossed over, and she sniffled. "I love you more than life itself, Della Marie, and I'm so proud of who you are." She dropped a kiss on my cheek. "The bus will be here soon," she reminded me. "Promise me you'll call when you get there, okay?"

"I promise." I threw my arms around her delicate frame and held her close, breathing in the scent of cinnamon and sugar. "I love you."

"I love you more," she whispered. We parted, and she helped me carry my luggage to the car before she drove me to the bus stop outside town. I didn't look back when I boarded that bus.

I wish I had.

What happens when Della moves back to Kiptsy Little Town eleven years later and Greer is the only one who can help her? When forced to be together, will the two final talk things out? Will Greer finally understand and accept why she needed to leave? Will Della regret breaking his heart?

Book 4 is now available!

Printed in Great Britain
by Amazon

19366798R00058